The men would be closing in on them.

"We need to get down to those cars."

Willow continued to shake her head. Though it had been Claude's decision to land and hers to make him stay in the chopper, thinking he'd be safer, guilt and shock washed over her, threatening to pull her under. A different choice might have caused Quentin to be killed.

He wrapped his arm around her and squeezed her shoulder, leading her toward the cover of the trees. He felt like he was almost carrying her. The shock from seeing yet another body, as well as the realization that they weren't going to get away easily from the men bent on murder, had probably sent her over the edge. "We've got to keep moving if we're going to stay alive."

The noise in the trees told him their pursuers were close. The gunshot shattering the air confirmed it.

Ever since she found the Nancy Drew books with the pink covers in her country school library, **Sharon Dunn** has loved mystery and suspense. Most of her books take place in Montana, where she lives with three nearly grown children and a hyper border collie. She lost her beloved husband of twenty-seven years to cancer in 2014. When she isn't writing, she loves to hike surrounded by God's beauty.

Books by Sharon Dunn

Love Inspired Suspense

Broken Trust
Zero Visibility
Montana Standoff
Top Secret Identity
Wilderness Target
Cold Case Justice
Mistaken Target
Fatal Vendetta
Big Sky Showdown
Hidden Away
In Too Deep
Wilderness Secrets
Mountain Captive
Undercover Threat
Alaskan Christmas Target
Undercover Mountain Pursuit

Alaska K-9 Unit

Undercover Mission

Visit the Author Profile page at LoveInspired.com for more titles.

UNDERCOVER MOUNTAIN PURSUIT

SHARON DUNN

LOVE INSPIRED SUSPENSE

INSPIRATIONAL ROMANCE

LOVE INSPIRED® SUSPENSE

INSPIRATIONAL ROMANCE

ISBN-13: 978-1-335-55482-6

Recycling programs
for this product may
not exist in your area.

Undercover Mountain Pursuit

This edition published by arrangement with Harlequin Books S.A.

For questions and comments about the quality of this book, please contact us at CustomerService@Harlequin.com.

Love Inspired
22 Adelaide St. West, 41st Floor
Toronto, Ontario M5H 4E3, Canada
www.LoveInspired.com

Printed in U.S.A.

He healeth the broken in heart,
and bindeth up their wounds.
—Psalm 147:3

I had fainted, unless I had believed to see the
goodness of the Lord in the land of the living.
—Psalm 27:13

For anyone who has lost a loved one
and fought their way back to the land of the living.

This book was conceived under a time of extreme stress,
when I sold the house I had lived in for twenty-eight
years. My load was lightened by a real estate agent
who went above and beyond what the job required
to help me. So, Denise, this book is dedicated to you.
Thank you for helping me transition into my new life.

ONE

Willow Farris leaned out the open door of the helicopter and drew her camera up to her eye. The whir of the blades, the warm mechanical hum of the engine, the feel of the safety harness holding her secure as she leaned even farther out so she was almost hanging in midair—it all made her adrenaline soar. This was the excitement that she lived for. Only the riskiest photography brought her satisfaction.

Last week she'd gotten an almost impossible shot of a grizzly bear. This week she was working for Vertical Limit, a stock photo company known for its shots of iconic places and hard-to-get photos. Though she traveled all over the world, this assignment was in her backyard. Vertical Limit wanted photos of iconic places in Wyoming and Montana. The remote waterfall Willow was photographing today was only a hundred miles from where she'd grown up.

She adjusted the focus on her lens. Two men stood beside a tall cliff with their backs to her. Water cascaded down the side of the mountain landing in a pool at the bottom.

The two men had been helicoptered into the remote

location in advance of her. One was a guide and the other a production coordinator.

She hadn't met the guide. She'd spoken briefly to the production coordinator, Henry Somebody. She didn't remember his last name.

She signaled the pilot to dip down as they drew closer. She took one shot after another. The second man turned and looked up toward her. Her heart skipped a beat. The first time she was seeing Quentin Decker since the accident was through her camera lens. What was he doing here? She moved the camera away from her eyes. Recognition spread across Quentin's face as well.

Five years ago, after the death of her brother, Luke, Quentin had left town and fallen off the face of the earth. They'd been high school sweethearts and engaged to be married. The car accident the three of them had been in had killed Luke. Their love for each other had not been strong enough to weather the grief, trauma and guilt.

"You all right?" the chopper pilot shouted above the whir of the blades. Claude was an older man who made his living flying tourists and hunters around the Montana wilderness. Willow considered him a friend. Her body language must have communicated her distress.

Trembling hands clutched the camera. For Quentin to return after five years felt almost cruel. Maybe it was just work that brought him back here, but why not get in touch with her? Her tight chest indicated that all the pain of the past had come back tenfold. "I'm just fine." Willow drew the camera back up to her eye, but what she saw through the lens was blurred by tears.

She swiped at her eyes. She had a job to do. She

dared not look down at Quentin, though she sensed he was watching her.

As they drew nearer to the waterfall, the pilot rose in elevation to avoid hitting the cliff. While he hovered, she took several more shots. Her camera whirred like a deck of cards being shuffled. Down below backpacks and cases were strewn around. Some of it contained more of her equipment. This location was accessible only by helicopter or by hiking in. The vehicles were parked miles down the mountain.

She leaned back and shouted to be heard above the noise of the helicopter. "Claude, can we turn back around? I want some shots from the opposite angle, coming back over the waterfall." She pulled her camera bag toward her and switched out her lens.

The pilot gave her the thumbs-up. "Gonna take a minute." Claude's thin white hair stuck out from beneath his headset.

He rose straight up above the cliff and glided over the rock plateau where the water flowed. Quentin and Henry were no longer visible. She checked the photos she'd already taken, picturing in her mind possibilities for unexpected shots. Quentin's face flashed across her screen. She hadn't realized she'd snapped a picture of him. Her throat went tight, and it felt like there was a weight on her chest. Why after five years with no contact did he have to come back here and turn her world upside down?

The pilot swung in a wide arc to get turned around. He looked to her for instruction.

She used hand signals to be understood as she shouted above the whir of the blades and the rumble of the engine. "Other side, quick drop down and a hover.

Then maybe back up and farther out. Then we'll land and I'll get some shots from the ground."

The pilot gave her another thumbs-up. She shifted so she could hang out the other side of the chopper. Once he got close to the edge of the cliff, Claude eased the chopper into position.

The chopper inched over the edge of the cliff. She was within ten feet of the waterfall. Her camera clicked off shot after shot. The helicopter turned slowly. In her peripheral vision, she could just see the ground where the two men had been standing. She craned her neck out the open door of the chopper, the wind hitting her face.

What she saw down below made her blood freeze. Shocked, she let go of her camera which hung by the neck strap. She almost couldn't comprehend what her eyes were telling her. Red. She saw red. Blood. Henry, the production coordinator, lay on his back. His face without color, a red spot spreading on his chest. From this distance, she did not know if he was alive or dead. She didn't see Quentin anywhere.

Two strange men. One of them with a gun. The other rooting through the equipment, tearing open backpacks and cases. Her breath caught in her throat.

The man with the gun looked toward the helicopter and then raised his weapon. He wore a yellow shirt. The pilot reacted by making a lateral move to avoid being shot. When she glanced out her door, the cliff face was only a few feet away. She saw movement flash in the trees, and the man in the yellow shirt headed in that direction.

The pilot sped away from where the violence had taken place. They were only inches from the treetops.

Feeling numb, she crawled toward the empty copilot chair. She gripped the back of the seat.

"We need to help those guys," said Claude.

She didn't know if Henry was still alive, or what had happened to Quentin.

The pilot's face had gone white and his hands were shaking. Claude was clearly in shock.

While she appreciated his heroic choice to stay and help, she wasn't sure he was up to the challenge. She knew he had a heart condition. She needed to protect him too.

He found an open area surrounded by forest and lowered the chopper to the ground.

"I'm going to see if I can save either of those two men."

"I'll go with you," said Claude. It was clear that he was not in any condition to help.

"Just radio local law enforcement. Let them know what happened here." Cell phones were useless this far away from a tower. The closest town was at least fifty miles away and probably didn't have EMTs or a hospital. Because the area was not accessible by car, it might take some time for help to show up. If Henry was still alive, they couldn't wait for help. They'd have to transport him themselves. She worried about what had happened to Quentin. Why had he disappeared?

Claude pulled his headset off and ran gnarled hands through his thin hair. "At least one of those strangers was armed."

Her heart raced as she slammed the clip into her gun. "I saw that." She could not begin to imagine what the men were doing in this remote location. They must have hiked in and then waited for their chance to attack. They were clearly looking for something.

The older man was still shaking. She patted his shoulder. "You stay here, Claude. Make that call. We may have to transport an injured man."

He nodded.

She tore her camera off her neck and jumped out of the chopper. Because her work was dangerous, especially when photographing wildlife, she carried a gun and pepper spray in her equipment bag. After grabbing them, she put them in one of her many pockets and then she sprinted through the trees. She slowed as she drew closer to the place where the violence had occurred.

Pushing the tree branch out of the way, she peered out at the area where Quentin and the other man had been. Henry lay the in same position as before. He hadn't moved at all. Most likely, he was dead. Her fear was so intense it felt like she was breathing through a straw.

Almost every container and case had been emptied or dumped out on the ground. There was some food and extra photo gear strewn all over. One of the backpacks was missing. She pulled her gun, waiting, watching and listening. The waterfall sang its soft symphony in the background.

She did not hear or see anything else. There was no movement or flashes of color in the nearby trees. A few minutes passed. Whoever those men were, they both must have gone deeper into the forest. Maybe they had found what they were looking for and left. Did she dare hope that? She had to move out with caution and assume they could come back at any minute.

Concern over what might have happened to Quentin washed over her as she studied the trees on the other side of the clearing.

She moved toward the man lying on the ground praying that she was wrong and that he was still alive. Even before she reached out to check for a pulse, she knew by how pale he was that Henry was dead. She shook her head, trying to get a deep breath and focus on what she needed to do to find Quentin and get out of there alive.

She had to think of Claude too with his heart condition. Maybe they should leave and bring help. But would Quentin survive?

A gunshot cracked somewhere in the forest. Her heart thudded as she lifted her head. Panic flooded her mind and body. One of the strangers must be taking shots at Quentin.

That answered her question as to what she needed to do. She ran in the direction the gunshot had come from.

Quentin Decker could hear the clumsy steps of his pursuer, a man in a yellow shirt. The shot had gone wild as the man tried to aim and run at the same time. Although Quentin didn't think he had been outed, this attack by these two men had to be connected to his undercover work. One of the two men had been rooting through things as though looking for something.

For two years, Quentin had been undercover trying to track an international theft ring. Artifacts, jewelry, artwork stolen from private collections and museums. Because the crimes were international, the investigation involved multiple agencies. His work was with the CIA.

Six months ago, they'd had their first big break. Anytime something was stolen, the photography agency he now was working for was in town on a shoot. There was no way Vertical Limit could be making enough money off stock photos to travel the world like they did. It had to be some sort of front. At the very least, the employees might be couriers for the stolen items.

Quentin sprinted through the trees and another shot was fired at him. This one was close enough to pummel his eardrum. The shooter's accuracy was improving. Quentin prayed the man in the yellow shirt would run out of bullets before he hit his target.

When Quentin had learned that the Vertical Limit company was going to be doing a photo shoot in an area where he'd grown up, he managed to get hired on as a freelance guide. It had been a shock to see his former fiancée, Willow, hanging out of that helicopter. She wasn't working as a photographer five years ago.

When he realized he'd be returning close to his hometown after so long his thoughts had turned to Willow, what they had shared together and how it had all been destroyed by the car accident that had killed her brother. His intention had been to get in touch with her when the investigation wasn't in high gear, not to catch her by surprise like he had.

He wasn't the same man who had run away from his pain and hers five years ago. Still, seeing her had been like an electric shock to his heart. He hoped she and the pilot were able to escape to a safe place.

As he ran through the forest, Quentin glanced over his shoulder. The man in the yellow shirt was still too close for comfort. He surged into a sprint deeper into the trees.

He had a theory about why they had been attacked in this remote location. With some effort, he'd been winning the trust of the production coordinator who had hinted at money troubles. Quentin wondered if maybe Henry was a courier for the smuggling ring and had decided to keep the stolen item and fence it himself for a bigger profit. The second attacker must have been looking for something, maybe the necklace that had been stolen from a villa in Italy weeks ago.

If he had only had a few more days to win Henry's trust, Henry might have confided in Quentin.

The men had shown up just as the helicopter had gone out of view. Were Willow and the pilot able to go for help? They were miles from anywhere.

He ran faster, jumping over a fallen tree and pushing branches out of his way. The noise behind him grew more distant. Though he was out of breath, he kept running. Maybe he could make it to where they'd parked the cars. Henry had been shot at point-blank range. Quentin knew he was dead before he hit the ground. Henry had mentioned a wife and child. Quentin said a prayer for them.

Behind him, he heard a thud and an expletive. He still hadn't shaken his pursuer. They really wanted to make sure there were no witnesses to the killing.

Quentin willed his legs to work harder, faster over the uneven terrain as he headed downhill. He was guessing at where the vehicles were. It might take a while to get to the cars. He'd been the one driving and was grateful he had the keys. Still, trying to start a car with someone shooting at him would be a challenge. He needed to shake this guy first.

He sprinted from one tree to the next in a zigzag pattern hoping to throw off Yellowshirt.

For at least five minutes, he ran without hearing anything from his pursuer. Had he managed to lose him? Quentin slipped behind a large tree trunk seeking to catch his breath and listen. The treetops swayed in the wind. A crow cawed in the distance.

When he closed his eyes, he saw images of Henry being shot and falling to the ground. His heart squeezed tight as another memory of unthinkable violence surfaced. His partner and mentor had been shot. Gunfire echoed through Quentin's head. The investigation into the smuggling ring had taken them to Italy when news of the theft of an expensive necklace had surfaced.

He remembered rounding the corner of the building in Italy. His footsteps pounding the cobblestone street. His partner lay on the ground. The crimson circle on his stomach growing as the older man pressed his hand against the fatal wound. David Stone had time to tell him that Mr. Smith, the man believed to be the head of the theft ring, had shot him. Little was known about him. It was speculated that he was European and changed his appearance often. David had lifted his bloody hand to his collarbone and said, *Dragonfly.* Meaning the man had a dragonfly tattoo. That was the sum total of what they knew about the elusive Mr. Smith.

Quentin pushed the memories out of his mind. He needed to get to those cars and off this mountain. Satisfied that he'd managed to shake his pursuer for now, he headed downhill, moving slower in order to be quiet. When he glanced over his shoulder all he saw was aspen trees. The round green leaves shook like coins in the wind.

Moving from tree to tree, he chose his steps carefully so as to not break any deadfall and draw attention to his position. He had a feeling the man with the gun would not give up easily if his orders were to leave no witnesses.

He stopped when he saw a flash of color in front of him. Had the guy managed to flank him? Quentin glanced around looking for a place to hide.

A branch broke. Willow emerged through the trees. The red laser dot of her handgun rested on his chest.

TWO

When she saw Quentin, she exhaled and let the gun fall at her side. "I thought you were that guy with the gun."

Quentin wrinkled his forehead as concern etched across his features. "What are you doing here? Why didn't you and the pilot get away and go for help?"

All the unresolved emotion over what had happened five years ago rose to the surface. "The pilot made the decision to land. I hoped that other man was still alive so we could transport him. I was worried about you."

"You didn't need to put yourself in that kind of danger."

"I have a gun. I can take care of myself." Which is what she'd been doing for the last five years. Thank you very much. She was aware enough to know the anger coming out was over the past and the way they had wounded each other. "Do you know what is going on here? Why was Henry shot?"

An emotion she could not read flickered across Quentin's face. What was he hiding?

A noise, perhaps a branch breaking, emanated from the trees behind them.

Quentin put his finger to his lips indicating that at least one of the attackers was still somewhere close. She barely had time to process what he'd communicated when a gunshot cracked the silence. As she turned to run, she registered flashes of movement in the trees coming toward them.

Quentin fell in beside her.

She spoke between breaths as she sprinted. "To the helicopter. We can get out of here."

She was used to danger, but not to death. They had to run, to get away. She had no idea why this had happened. Quentin had not had time to offer an explanation.

Quentin kept pace with her. Though she was a little lost by the sameness of the landmarks, mostly aspens and some evergreens, she knew the general direction they needed to go. At least Quentin had not been shot. She still could not understand why such horrible violence would happen. Drugs maybe? Was that what the other man had been searching for? Maybe the two men had been waiting for the opportunity to kill Henry in an isolated place. And now it was clear the killers wanted to make sure that the only witnesses were eliminated.

That meant she and Quentin would be hunted until they were dead. Not if she could help it. She ran faster. Several minutes passed without any sign of the man in the yellow shirt.

Quentin glanced side to side. "Are we going in the right direction?"

She slowed down to a jog, taking in her surroundings. "If we can get close to the waterfall, I can orient us to the helicopter."

Quentin stopped. He turned one way then tilted his

head toward the sky. He pointed off to the left. "I think we need to be going in this direction."

She stopped to catch her breath. Normally, she was good at finding her way through the wilderness. The shock of gunfire and seeing a dead man had traumatized her and made it hard to think clearly.

Another gunshot sounded behind them, a reminder that they were still being pursued. Flashes of yellow indicated the man was running through the trees toward them, closing the distance. Less than twenty yards away.

She lifted her own gun and fired a shot knowing she wouldn't have accuracy on a moving target at that distance but intending to scare and slow down her pursuer. She couldn't see the man with the gun anymore through the trees. The gunfire had been effective. He must have stopped or at least was moving toward them with greater caution.

"Why don't you let me have the gun?" asked Quentin.

Why did he want her gun? "I'll hold on to it. Thanks."

She wondered what Quentin had been doing for the last five years. He'd been a deputy before he left Montana, but maybe he had fallen on the wrong side of the law. She knew him well enough to know he was keeping secrets. Could she even trust him?

The sound of breaking branches behind them interrupted her racing thoughts.

They took off running. She followed Quentin's lead as he changed direction and pushed through some thick undergrowth. The man in the yellow shirt stayed close at first. Quentin disappeared into the thick of the trees. She struggled to keep up, willing herself to go faster. She kept running though she'd lost sight of Quentin.

When she looked over her shoulder, the man in the yellow shirt was getting closer. To shake him, she wove through the trees.

She came to a clearing. Now she was really lost. In an effort to escape the man with the gun, she'd veered away from Quentin. Certainly, Quentin must have wondered what happened to her. Her heart beat a little faster. Quentin was the only one left alive. What if he was somehow connected to those two men? Her hand slipped into her pocket where she kept the short barrel .38. Quentin's interest in taking her gun had alarmed her. Maybe he'd ditched her on purpose. Maybe she should assume she was on her own and that all three men were after her. She didn't want to think that of the man she'd once loved. His betrayal in leaving when she needed him most five years ago affected her perception of him now.

She ran in the general direction of the waterfall. The trees thinned. She could see the top of the cliff face and hear the waterfall that less than an hour ago she'd photographed. Now she knew where she was. She hurried through the forest but slowed down as she drew closer to where the body of the dead man was. She heard noise. She crept forward. Even before she had a visual, she knew the other attacker was back rooting through things again. He hadn't found what he was looking for yet.

Using the trees as cover, she peered out. She hadn't expected the man to be so close. He was less than ten feet away dumping out the contents of a different backpack. He must have sensed someone staring at him. He looked up. She saw his face. His shirt was unbuttoned revealing a dragonfly tattoo on his chest.

The man looked right at her. The moment of eye

contact sent a chill through her. She had a near photographic memory. That face was etched in her mind. On instinct, she darted back deeper into the cover of the forest. Too late. He was after her.

A shot was fired in her direction. So Dragonfly had a gun too. She whirled around and headed back into the forest. How was she going to get to that chopper? She'd have to do a wide arc around the waterfall with Dragonfly hot on her heels. She feared she was running straight toward the man in the yellow shirt.

Another shot was fired. The brush got thicker. She slowed down knowing she had a degree of cover and that it would be better to be quiet with Dragonfly so close. She slipped behind a leafy bush. Her heart pounded as footsteps, slow and deliberate, came toward her.

She peered through the bush. It was Dragonfly. He wore distinct new-looking hiking boots. The man turned his back and continued to search. Now was her chance. She pulled the gun from her pocket and lifted it. She aimed to injure not kill.

"There you are." A voice off to her side distracted her. The man with the tattoo was alerted as well. His back stiffened, then he walked toward where the voice had come from. That must be Yellowshirt. She could hear two voices now. The attackers were talking. She caught only snippets of the conversation. One said something about a wild-goose chase and getting lost. The other said something about not leaving until everyone was dead.

The words sent a shudder through her. Her palms grew cold and clammy.

A hand went over her mouth while the other reached for her gun.

* * *

With the two killers so close, Quentin had to make sure Willow didn't scream out of fear when he came up behind her. Plus, she was holding a gun. When she stopped struggling, he took his hand off her mouth. She turned around. She still held the gun aimed at the sky. He put his finger to his lips indicating she needed to be quiet. He crouched low so the bushes would provide them with cover. She put the gun back in her pocket as she kneeled facing him.

The two men were still talking, though it sounded like they were moving away from where he and Willow were.

Quentin turned back, furrowing his forehead and pointing, hoping that his mime act would communicate that she needed to show him which direction to go to reach the helicopter.

She shook her head, probably not understanding what he meant or maybe she didn't think it was a good idea to make a run for it yet.

The sound of footsteps and twigs breaking indicated that at least one of the attackers was moving toward where they were hidden by the brush.

Willow and Quentin crouched facing each other. Willow pressed her lips together. Her neck pulsed from her rapid heartbeat. Seeing her so close, those wide brown eyes, brought back memories he'd tried to run from for five years. He'd been the one driving the night of the accident. The guilt had eaten him alive. On the night he left town after the accident, they had had a fight. She told him to leave, that she didn't love him anymore. The pain her words caused felt brand-new when he was this close to her.

The footsteps seemed to be moving away from where they were hidden, but Quentin could still hear the man as he searched for his targets.

They waited, not moving, still as statues. Quentin pushed some of the brush out of the way and peered out. He couldn't see either of the men.

Every minute or so he heard a noise that indicated one of the men was within a few feet of them but then seemed to always to circle away from them. Still the man didn't leave the area.

His heart beat a little faster. The sun was still intense enough to cause sweat to form on his forehead. His muscles started to cramp from crouching. It sounded like the pursuer was beating the bushes with a stick. Quentin was grateful they were both dressed in colors that provided a degree of camouflage.

Willow's hand rested over the pocket where she kept that gun. The barrel was so short, it would only be accurate at close range. He'd feel more comfortable if he was the one with a weapon, but taking a gun with him meant he risked blowing his cover if it was found on him. He wasn't sure why Willow had acted suspicious when he'd asked for her gun. Did she not trust him?

He had no reason to believe his cover had been blown. Linking the photo agency to the smuggling had taken two years of work and had cost his partner his life. What would happen to the investigation after this, he had no idea. His superiors might make the decision to pull him out altogether. He hoped not. He wanted to close this case and take down the man who had killed his partner, and then he was getting out.

After he left Montana, the undercover assignments had been appealing. His previous experience in law enforcement made him a good candidate for the CIA. It helped him forget the pain. For a time, he'd lost himself in the work. Staying on the move, pretending to be someone else had been an escape from the pain of the past.

Right now, he needed to focus on getting out of here alive. Willow gasped. The man in the yellow shirt was separating the bushes close to them with his stick. He was within feet of where they were hiding. He must have stuffed the gun in a holster or pocket.

Two against one.

Quentin shout whispered to Willow, "Jump him."

Both of them burst up at the same time. The man had time to draw his gun and point it at Willow, who had already pulled her gun out.

Quentin lunged at the man just as a shot was fired. The bullet went up rather than toward Willow, but the noise would alert the other killer if he was close. With the two men in hand-to-hand combat, it would be hard for Willow to take a shot and risk hitting Quentin.

Quentin wrestled with the man who clung to the weapon and fired again. This time he heard a scream from Willow. Her gun lay on the ground. He didn't know if she'd been hit or just frightened enough to drop the gun.

Once the other killer showed up, they wouldn't have a chance.

Quentin held on to the other man's hand but could not wrench the pistol free. He squeezed the nerves in the man's wrist. Yellowshirt let go of the gun, but it fell into the bushes. A shot was fired somewhere in the trees. The second man was close, and he too was armed. Quentin hit the man in the yellow shirt on the side of the head. He crumpled to the ground. He was not unconscious, only struggling to recover from the blow. It bought them the time they needed to get away.

He didn't know if Willow had had time to pick up her gun or not.

They sprinted as the trees grew farther apart. In his peripheral vision, he could see the cliff and waterfall where the photos had been taken. Trees and brush hid the view of the murder scene.

Willow ran faster. She must have figured out where they were and could lead them to the chopper. A quick glance over his shoulder revealed they were being pursued by at least one man, though he was some distance behind them.

Willow ran into a clearing and he followed. She made a whirling gesture with her hand in the air which must mean they were close to the chopper.

The first hint that something was wrong was when the chopper blades and engine didn't roar to life once they would have been visible to the pilot.

Willow got to the chopper first. Her gasp was audible as she drew her hand up to her mouth. Her face went white. He peered inside. The pilot lay slumped to one side, a bullet through his temple. Quentin leaned in and grabbed the radio. The cord had been cut.

She shook her head. "No."

The men would be closing in on them. "We need to get down to those cars."

She continued to shake her head.

Quentin wrapped his arm around her and squeezed her shoulder, leading her toward the cover of the trees. He felt like he was almost having to carry her. The shock from seeing yet another body, as well as the realization that they weren't going to get away easily from the men bent on murder, had probably sent her over the edge. "We've got to keep moving if we're going to stay alive."

The noise in the trees told him their pursuer was close. The gunshot shattering the air confirmed it.

THREE

Willow's heartbeat drummed in her ears as her knees buckled. If it wasn't for Quentin's arm around her pulling her toward the trees, she wouldn't have been able to move at all.

Though it had been Claude's decision to land and hers to make him stay in the chopper thinking he'd be safer, guilt and shock washed over her, threatening to pull her under. What if they had just taken off and gone for help? They might not have gotten back in time to save Quentin. And she had not known if Henry was dead or alive. It was a tough call no matter what.

Seeing Claude dead had caused her to go over the edge. Until then, she had had hope. Were they going to escape these assassins? Why was this happening?

Though he was right beside her, holding her, Quentin's voice seemed very far away. "Willow, we have to run."

She felt like she was on autopilot as her legs pumped, and her feet hit the ground. Tree branches and sunlight flashed around her. Though he probably could have gone faster, Quentin stayed close to her. The terrain opened up to what looked like an overgrown trail. The pounding of her own footsteps seemed to break through her paralysis. There was no time to look over her shoulder. She had to assume they were being pursued.

After they'd run for some time, Quentin grabbed her and directed her off the trail. He must have seen something. Now they were moving down a hillside. The ground was hard and rocky. The trees were the shorter twisted trunk junipers instead of the tall evergreens and aspens.

Quentin grabbed her hand and squeezed. "This way. We need to hide."

His touch cleared her head even more. She craned her neck but saw nothing on the trail they had just left. He jogged toward a cluster of the short trees and fell to the ground behind them.

She followed. The trees did not provide much cover. She pressed close to him, so their shoulders were touching. Both of them were out of breath.

She whispered, "Are you hoping they pass by?"

He leaned close and whispered in her ear while he peered through the branches of the trees up the hill, "Yes, they should move past. It will buy us some time. I have only a vague idea of how to get back to those cars."

Just this morning, she'd parked her car and waited for the helicopter to return to transport her and her equipment. It felt like it had happened a hundred years ago. "It's hard to say where the cars are. We both saw the landscape from the air."

Quentin turned his head one way and then the other. "There were landmarks, mountain peaks. If we could get to an open area, we might be able to figure it out."

When she glanced around, everything looked the same. Her work took her into all kinds of environments, urban and remote. Someone else was usually doing the navigating, so she could focus on getting the shots she wanted. "Help should be coming for us. I told the pilot to radio about what had happened. I hope he was able to do that before…" Her voice trailed off. She did not want to think about what had happened to Claude.

Quentin's body jerked. "Quiet." He pressed lower to the ground.

She peered out through the crooked branches, seeing nothing. The makeshift trail they'd been on was not visible. When she listened, a distant pounding that might be footfalls reached her ears. Quentin tensed. He must've seen or heard something.

The seconds passed as the sound of her own breathing surrounded her. The hard ground pushed against her stomach. She was aware of the warmth of Quentin's shoulder as it pressed against hers. As they waited, his breathing seemed to augment in the silence.

She could not hear or see anything that indicated where the two men with guns were. She'd have to trust Quentin's judgment that it wasn't okay for them to move or talk yet. She felt guilty about her earlier suspicion of him. It was clear he wanted to protect her.

Quentin let out a breath and relaxed—actions that indicated he thought they had evaded the two pursuers. "I think it is safe for us to move now." He responded to what she had said minutes ago. "Do we know for sure the pilot was able to call for help? The radio was sabotaged. Unless there is a highway patrolman close who could be dispatched, if law enforcement is coming at all, it's probably from some town hours away."

Willow looked into Quentin's blue eyes, not sure how to respond to what he'd just said. Though he wasn't being unrealistic, his assessment of the situation made her even more afraid. "I guess we have no way of knowing if help is coming or not."

His expression softened. "It's not hopeless. If we work together, we'll get out of here alive."

His use of the word *together* caused a tightness in her rib cage. "I hope you're right. Quentin. Why did you come back here? Do you know something about who those men are?"

"Now is the not the time talk about this." He turned his attention back to where he'd been watching for the men.

Her muscles tensed. The old wounds that being close to Quentin brought to the surface had to be put on the back burner if they were going to survive.

He pushed himself to his feet and looked around. "We've got maybe five minutes before those two men deduce that we left the trail, and then they will start to backtrack. Let's head through those trees. Hopefully things will open up and we can figure out how to get to the parked cars."

They rose and sprinted through the open grassy area where they could be easily spotted, not slowing down until they were in the thick of the evergreens.

They ran for what felt like an hour, and still they were surrounded by forest.

She stopped to catch her breath. "I wish I would have thought to grab water and food."

Quentin halted and checked one of his pockets. He handed her a packet filled with liquid. "It's high-octane water, supposed to hydrate you faster than normal water."

"Thank you." She clicked open the resealable pouch. "Do you want some?"

"Sure."

She took several gulps and then handed it back to him. They kept walking until the sun was past the midway point, late afternoon. The terrain changed very little as they moved through the trees. Though it was spring, the temperature had started to drop as the day went on.

She wondered if help was coming at all. Maybe law enforcement had made it to the scene of the murders but had no idea where they needed to be looking for Quentin and her. If Claude had gotten through, he would have told them how many people were alive.

The water had helped with her thirst and did seem to give her a boost of energy. She was grateful they'd seemed to have shaken their pursuers for now.

"This is getting us nowhere," said Quentin. "I'm going to climb a tree and find out if I can see any landmark that would help us navigate." Quentin looked around until he spotted a tree with thick enough branches to hold him.

He moved up the tree with ease.

She stood at the base, holding her breath when he perched on a thinner branch toward the top. Her breath caught as it creaked and bent beneath his weight. He clung to the trunk with both hands. He didn't have a lot of faith in the limb holding him either.

"Can you see anything?"

"Yes, I can tell you right now we're really off course," Quentin said.

"But we can get to the cars?"

He peered down at her. "Let me come down and talk to you. I don't think talking loud is a great idea."

His comment reminded her that they were still being hunted.

He climbed down the tree and stood beside her. "I can see the mountain peak that was visible when we parked the cars. This stretch of forest ends in another half mile. Let's push through it."

"How far off track are we?"

"I'd say we're not going to get there before nightfall."

"That far?" She couldn't hide her frustration.

"Let's not waste any more time." They took off at a jog through the trees. When the forest opened up into a meadow, she could see the mountain peak Quentin had referenced.

He pointed off in the distance. "You can't see it from here, but the road where we parked the cars is directly below that peak."

"I'm just glad you were paying attention." She'd been focused on making sure all her camera gear was in order.

"Comes with living out in the country. You just get into the habit of paying attention to natural landmarks."

Quentin's family ranch was about a hundred miles from where they were. She wanted to ask him where he had been for the last five years, but the words caught in her throat. Even though she wanted to know and she felt she deserved an explanation, visiting the painful past would make it hard to function.

He sped up into a jog. "Let's try to get there before dark."

As they ran, she heard a whirring sound that was different from the wind. Quentin slowed his pace. It took her a moment to realize it was a helicopter she could hear but not see yet.

She searched the sky feeling a sense of relief. "A rescue helicopter?"

Quentin watched the sky as well as the whirring grew louder. "Maybe. It makes sense police would show up in a chopper given the location. But this area is nothing but small towns. Where would they get a helicopter so quickly? The pilot who took us up told me Vertical Limit booked him over a month ago."

She shuddered at the memory of Claude slumped over with a bullet through his head. Her throat squeezed tight. It would take a long time to get past all she had seen today.

The noise of the approaching helicopter caused them to look up at the clouds again. Her stomach clenched. How would a rescue helicopter know to look for them so far away from where the killings had happened? Still, she couldn't give up hope. The chopper came into view and drew closer. She was prepared to run or to wave her arms.

Fear ricocheted through her when the helicopter was close enough to see it clearly.

It was the chopper she'd been in hours before, and it was headed straight for them.

Quentin turned, assessing the fastest way to get to some cover. One of the murderers must also be a pilot. The men probably figured out he and Willow wouldn't be found on foot and had gone back for the chopper. Or at least one of them had. He couldn't see from this distance if both men were in the chopper or not.

Quentin and Willow sprinted toward the trees on the other side of the meadow as the chopper bore down on them. The whir of the blades grew louder, more intense.

Willow stumbled and fell. He leaned over to help her

up. A gunshot whizzed past his shoulder. The chopper hovered above them.

"Split up," he said. Two targets were harder to hit than one.

They veered apart. At least this way one of them had a chance of making it to the cover of the trees. The killer had only a handgun which meant he'd have to be really close to shoot with any accuracy. Quentin could see Willow headed toward the edge of the forest out of the corner of his eye.

The chopper engine sounded different. He peered over his shoulder. The helicopter hovered in the meadow maybe ten feet off the ground. Yellowshirt jumped out. The other man, the one he hadn't seen up close, must be the pilot. So, they would be hunted on the ground and from the air. Quentin turned his attention back to where he needed to be: in the cover of the trees. Noises behind him indicated that the helicopter was rising off the ground.

Quentin entered the safety of the forest, searching for Willow. The chopper was right above him. It was just a matter of seconds before the man on the ground would reach the trees as well. Gasping for breath, Quentin kept running, all the time looking for Willow.

He thought he saw movement in his peripheral vision, but it might be the shooter on the ground. He slowed down. Moving with caution and seeking cover seemed like the better option.

The chopper hovered over him, so close to the tree-tops that the intense wind created by the blades bent the top branches as it swept over back and forth.

He ran from tree to tree, bush to bush, well aware of how hopeless the situation had become now that their pursuers were utilizing the helicopter. It would be nothing for the man in the chopper to land where the cars were and wait for Quentin and Willow to show up.

The two murderers must have left their car somewhere too. He wondered where their car was. There weren't that many ways up the mountain or places to park on the treacherous road.

Quentin slipped behind a tree with a thick trunk. He pressed his back against the roughness of the bark. He took in air, trying to catch his breath while he listened and watched. He didn't see any sign of Willow, but he didn't hear any gunshots either. Maybe she too had found a hiding place and was waiting for the right moment to make a run for it.

He fought off a sense of defeat as he tried to come up with a strategy that would get him and Willow down the mountain without being killed. Above him, the helicopter moved in a circle, never leaving the area where he was hiding. The treetops probably provided enough cover to conceal him. Once he started moving, he'd be easier to spot from above in open areas. And it was possible that the man on foot would locate him as well.

He needed to find Willow and come up with a plan for their survival. True, the helicopter could beat them to where the cars were. And it was the most obvious place for him and Willow to go. The man in the helicopter couldn't be two places at once. Maybe they could get to the killers' car while the helicopter waited for them at the other cars. He shook his head. There were too many unknowns.

The helicopter noise grew more distant. The pilot was searching another part of the forest. Quentin took the opportunity to run deeper into the forest, moving in the general direction of the mountain peak. Any plan he came up with seemed doomed to fail. Unless he and Willow could find a way to at least catch and disable Yellowshirt, the situation seemed hopeless. But first he had to find Willow.

They hadn't been that far apart when they'd entered the shelter of the trees. It was concerning to him that he had not seen any sign of her yet. He prayed she was safe and that they would find each other. They were more vulnerable separated.

FOUR

Since entering the forest, Willow kept running. Though he had not yet caught up with her, Yellowshirt remained close. Every time she thought she'd shaken him, she'd hear noises that indicated otherwise.

Her legs were fatigued from the chase, and she was out of breath. Her pursuer, on the other hand, didn't seem to slow down at all. As she moved, she searched for a hiding place that wouldn't end up being her grave. She saw nothing but thin trees. Not even a fallen log to take cover behind.

She willed herself to run faster as she wove through the forest hoping that would make it harder to track her. In an effort to get away and stay alive, she had lost all sense of direction. It felt like she was still moving toward the mountain peak that Quentin said would help them find the parked cars. She spurred herself into a sprint despite the muscle soreness. Gasping for air, she kept going. She moved with intensity, hearing only the drumming of her heartbeat in her ears and the pounding of her footfalls.

When she thought her lungs would collapse, she

slowed down, wheezing in air. She slowed even more, not by choice but because she was spent.

She heard no noise that indicated her pursuer was anywhere close. Maybe she had finally put enough distance between herself and Yellowshirt. She jogged rather than sprinted. All she heard was the wind rustling the leaves above her. She heard the faint sound of the helicopter. So he was still searching but was no longer close. Still, she needed to be on her guard. The chopper could circle back very quickly.

She wondered why she had not seen or heard Quentin since they'd entered the forest. She stepped over some fallen branches and took a deep breath.

Out of nowhere, a gunshot echoed around her. Her whole body jerked from the sound. She reached for her own gun just as a weight slammed into her back.

She screamed in pain as her body was pushed to the ground with tremendous force.

"Thanks a lot. I'm out of bullets." The attacker put his full weight on her torso, pinning her to the ground. "Give me your gun, now."

"I can't reach it. I can't move." Each word was forced. His weight on her made it hard to breathe. "Please, you have to let me turn over. It's in my front pocket."

There was a moment's hesitation as if the man was thinking over his options. "You stay still. Keep your hands where I can see them. Which pocket is it in?"

"My left."

The weight lifted off her back. She was well aware that once the man took the gun, her life was over.

"Hands above you before you roll over."

She complied. And then rolled over. The man reached toward her left pocket. She lifted her leg. Her knee collided with the underside of his chin. Blood flowed out of the culprit's mouth. He must have bitten his tongue. She saw his face clearly. This man was not the one with the dragonfly tattoo. He was the one who must have done most of the shooting while the other man searched through things.

Rage flashed across his features as he leaned toward Willow. A fist came toward her face. She twisted her body to avoid impact. The man grabbed her hair when she turned sideways. His free hand fumbled around her pocket. He let go of her hair.

She flipped on her back and drew her legs up to her chest. He had the gun pointed at her as he stood in a kneeling position over her. She landed a blow with both feet to his stomach. He doubled over. She sat up and reached for her gun as he gripped it.

They wrestled. The gun got dropped. He hit her in the stomach twice which weakened and disoriented her. He reached down to wrap his hands around her neck. She fought to get away and clawed at his fingers.

Thud. Smack.

The pressure on her throat stopped. Quentin stood over them holding a thick branch. Yellowshirt was disabled but not unconscious. He lay on his stomach. Groaning and wiggling, he propped himself on his elbows.

Still standing over the man and holding the stick in a defensive position, Quentin glanced around. "If we had some way to tie this guy up..."

Willow pushed herself to her feet but swayed and blinked. Lightheaded from the fight, she glanced around for her gun but didn't see it.

The killer had blood coming out of his mouth as he pulled himself to his hands and knees.

She reached down to remove her laces from her hiking boots to tie him up.

The intense wind and a mechanical hum above them changed the plan. The man in the helicopter drew closer. They were in an open enough area to be easy targets. The chopper dropped even lower to the ground. The setting sun obscured the man's face, but light glinted off the gun he held propped on the rim of the helicopter window to steady it.

The other man had gotten to his feet and lifted his fist above his head intending to hit Willow. Quentin blocked the blow with his branch and grabbed Willow, indicating that running was probably the best option.

With the whir and clang of the helicopter seemingly right on top of them, they headed toward where the trees were thicker.

Willow was grateful that Quentin had shown up when he did, otherwise she might not have lived. They kept running. Eventually, the noise of the chopper grew fainter. The man in the chopper was probably trying to figure out where they would appear.

When the trees thinned, she caught glimpses of the mountain peaks. They ran for what felt like hours, stopping only to catch their breath. The sun slipped down low on the horizon. The sky grew gray.

The chopper didn't get closer, though they could hear it fading and then growing louder, always searching. They didn't hear or see any sign of the man on foot, but they had to assume he was still after them. He'd probably taken the time to look for her gun.

Quentin stopped her when the trees thinned out. In the fading light, she could see the mountain peak. Flashing lights off in the distance indicated where the chopper was.

"Do you think he'll just touch down and wait for us to show up at those cars?"

"It makes the most sense," said Quentin. He slumped to the ground, using a tree trunk as a back rest.

"We should keep going. That other guy is probably still looking for us. He may have found my gun."

"Rest a bit. Once we're out in the open, the chopper can spot us easily. If we wait until it's darker, we have a better chance."

Willow was beyond exhausted. She'd been running on fear-fueled adrenaline. She slumped down beside Quentin. "Even if we get to those cars, it doesn't mean we'll be able to escape, does it? Not if the man in the chopper gets there first."

Quentin tilted his head up toward the sky. She could still hear the faint hum of the chopper. "Once it's totally dark, he won't be able to see which way we're going."

She closed her eyes. "It's strange we haven't heard or seen the guy on the ground. He wasn't having trouble tracking us before."

"Yeah, that concerns me. He might have gotten back in the chopper," Quentin said.

"What are we going to do, Quentin?" For the first time since she'd seen the dead man from the chopper, the sense of hopelessness returned. Were they going to die on this mountain?

The note of despair in Willow's voice pierced through him. She was innocent in all of this, and yet she'd been drawn into it and her life was under threat.

She shook her head. "What is this all about anyway? Why did Henry and Claude have to die?"

"Hard to say." Quentin wished he could tell her more, but he couldn't risk blowing his cover. When they'd been face-to-face with the killer in the yellow shirt on the ground, he recognized him as one of the thieves connected to the smuggling ring which only confirmed his suspicions.

Willow shook her head. "Just this morning I was so excited about this assignment. I like jobs that test me physically, but not ones where I have to run for my life." She rested her face in her hands. Her jerking shoulders indicated she was crying.

His heart filled with compassion. He wrapped an arm around her. "All of this has been beyond horrifying, but I believe we can get out of here. We have to."

She lifted her head and turned to face him. Her faltering voice cut through him. "Why is this happening? Who are those men? Do you know something, Quentin?"

Quentin's throat went dry. He didn't want to lie to her. Best not to say anything at all. He drew her closer in a sideways hug.

He held her while she cried. Having her so close brought back memories of what they had shared. All through high school and up until the accident, he, Luke and Willow had been inseparable, calling themselves the three musketeers while they skied, rock climbed and hung out at his family ranch together. It wasn't until he'd gotten his job as a deputy that he realized that what he felt for Willow was deeper than friendship. Luke had been like a brother to him. With a single jerk of the steering wheel all of that had been destroyed.

She rested her head against his shoulder and slept. The sky turned from gray to black. In the time they slept and waited for the cover of darkness, he didn't hear the helicopter at all. His best guess was that the chopper had landed close to the parked cars and was waiting for them to show up. The chopper would eventually run out of fuel, so it couldn't keep flying around searching forever.

Quentin leaned his head back and dozed. When he opened his eyes, the stars twinkled above him. The night sky reminded him of his childhood growing up on a ranch far from city lights. How much time had passed? Hours?

Willow pulled away from his shoulder. "Wow, I must have been really tired."

"Me too," he said. "We have the cover of night. Let's see if we can get out of here."

"How close do you think we are to those cars?"

He glanced in the direction of the mountain peak that helped orient him. "Four or five miles maybe." He had no way of knowing what the terrain was like in between where they were and the cars.

Quentin started walking, and she fell in beside him. Their footsteps created a rhythm. He wanted to know more about who she had become since he'd been gone. The truth was when he held her, he realized how much he'd missed her. "What made you take up the high-risk photography?" She had been working as a waitress and ski instructor when he left town.

She didn't answer at first. They treaded slowly with no light to illuminate their path.

"I sort of fell into it, and then I found out I was good at it. I've traveled all over the world. They need someone to follow an extreme skier down a mountain, they call me. They need someone to trek through the jungle to get a picture of a rare bird, they call me."

"Sounds like a rush."

"I like the excitement factor," she said. "I might ask you what you've been doing for the last five years." Her words were filled with anguish.

Again, he hated not being able to tell her what he was doing back so close to where he'd grown up. "I'm not sure what to say, Willow. Lots of water under the bridge between us. I didn't come back here to hurt you again. Please know that."

She let out an exasperated breath. "Why come back at all?" Anger had crept into her voice.

"I don't blame you for being angry."

"You don't blame me?" She stopped and faced him. "You left me when I needed you the most."

Her words were like a knife through his heart. He was transported back to when he felt so helpless and so guilt ridden that he had run from the intense feelings. "I know. I'm sorry." He wanted to tell her that he had grown in their years apart. He had come to a place of forgiving himself for overcorrecting when he was driving the car that killed Luke. Willow was still in so much pain. Now was not the time to try to work through it. Maybe God had brought him back here for more than just his work.

They walked in silence for a while longer. Only the moon and stars lighted their way. They were in a grassy open area with a few trees.

They came to what looked like a very primitive road. Plant life had grown over it.

"Where do you suppose it leads?"

"It's probably an old logging road," he said. "Hard to say where it goes."

"What if we followed it? It must go somewhere," she said.

"It could be a dead-end or only lead to some broken-down cabin no one lives in. This could have been used a hundred years ago."

Her disappointment was palpable.

"I appreciate that you are trying to find another way for us to get out of here. I just don't know if this is our best choice," he said.

As they continued to walk, his mind considered their options. The drive up the mountain road before they had to be transported by helicopter to the sight had taken over two hours. Even if they kept up a good pace, it would be early morning before they made it down the mountain. At the base of the mountain was a country road where there probably wasn't much traffic in the predawn hours. If a car did go by, there was a chance the driver would be suspicious of two people wandering in such a remote place and not stop at all.

"I still think we should try to get to one of those cars and drive out of here. We know how to locate them."

She shook her head. "The guy in the helicopter could've sabotaged the cars so they won't run."

His clenched his jaw. She was right about that.

Before Quentin had a chance to answer, headlights appeared in front of them, maybe twenty yards away. The vehicle came toward them at a high speed. Heart racing, Quentin wrapped his arms around Willow and directed her away from the path.

The car veered off the road and continued to bear down on them. They needed to get into the thick of the trees where the car couldn't go. Willow sprinted. He followed her. Once they were under the canopy of the trees, it grew even darker. They slowed their pace.

Behind him he heard a car door slam. Bright light through the trees illuminated a wide swath of the forest. He and Willow ran faster to get to where the darkness hid them. The killer had a very powerful flashlight. It was clear now why they hadn't heard or seen Yellowshirt for some time. He'd gone to get a car, probably his own which had a flashlight and maybe even more weapons. The helicopter may have taken him there to save time. Most likely, he had found Willow's gun as well.

Quentin's theory was confirmed when the first gunshots echoed through the forest. He could hear but not see Willow as she ran. He veered toward her, not wanting them to be separated again.

As they were pursued, the light shone on them again and more shots were fired. They both ran off to the side which led them away from the mountain peak. The killer had left the car out on the makeshift road. Could they double back and get to it before Yellowshirt figured out what they were doing and cut them off or shot them?

It was worth a try.

Willow followed him. After they'd run for five minutes, they could see the light flashing through the trees still coming toward them, but they had put some distance between themselves and the killer.

Quentin turned again, this time moving to the west. After they'd run for a while the land opened up and he could orient himself. A few minutes later, they were on the makeshift road again. He didn't see the car anywhere. When he peered over his shoulder, no light was flashing through the trees. That was a little concerning. Maybe the killer had figured out their plan and gone back to his car.

They hurried uphill and rounded a curve where he thought the car would be, but instead, he saw only more of the rutty, overgrown road. Both of them slowed. They'd gone farther downhill than he'd realized.

"We have to keep going," said Willow. "Finding that car is our best shot at getting out of here."

She patted his shoulder and kept going.

He saw the parked car. A second later he spotted the flashing lights through the forest headed toward the vehicle. They had only seconds to get to the car before Yellowshirt did. Despite painful muscle fatigue Quentin bolted toward the car.

He reached the driver's side door which faced the forest and the killer's light. Three gunshots echoed through the forest. Glass in the driver's side window shattered and sprayed. He flung the door open and crawled into the driver's seat. He said a prayer of thanks when he saw the keys in the ignition.

Willow had gotten into the passenger seat and slipped down low beneath the window. Broken glass pressed into his legs as he did the same thing while he started the car.

Another shot was fired, this time glancing off the windshield. As he emerged from the forest, the killer stood off to the side but in front of them. The windshield splintered but didn't shatter.

Quentin floored the gas pedal. Jerking the wheel, he veered as far away from their armed pursuer as he could. The car to bounced on the uneven terrain. The killer managed to fire two more shots, one of which hit the back window.

Quentin kept up the dangerous speed in an effort to get to the curve in the road that would provide a degree of protection. When he checked the rearview mirror, the glow of the flashlight indicated the killer was running toward them.

As he turned the wheel into the curve, the car jerked and caught air, landing with a jarring motion that made his teeth slam together. Even though he was pretty sure the man had given up, the adrenaline surging through him made it hard to slow the car down.

Willow gripped the seat rest between them. "I sure don't want to die in a rollover."

Quentin let up on the gas a little. "Sorry." His memory flashed on another time he'd been driving. His voice softened. "So sorry. I didn't mean to scare you."

Her body relaxed. She looked over her shoulder. "I think we're in the clear."

He took in a ragged breath as the realization sank in. "We did get away, didn't we?" The path in front of him had ridges and clumps of plants and grass and small twig-like trees.

"Let's hope this road takes us somewhere."

"It has to. How else could they have gotten up here? It must connect with a real road." Right now, what they were traveling on wasn't so much a road as a path between the trees. He drove for another ten minutes. The road smoothed out, became less treacherous. It certainly wasn't the road they'd taken this morning to get up here.

"We have to run into something sooner or later, right?" Doubt clouded Willow's words.

Quentin nodded and peered through the windshield that had spider vein cuts all through it.

They drove for at least twenty minutes. The road

seemed to wind through the countryside in an aimless sort of way. The landscape opened up and there were fewer trees. Still they didn't encounter any connecting roads. What choice did they have but to keep driving?

They had a quarter tank of gas.

Willow must have felt uneasy as well. She kept looking through her window and then the back one, probably trying to find something that looked familiar.

It was still dark out. Shrouded in shadow, the area looked very different from when they had come up here in the early morning hours.

With the tank close to empty, he pulled off on the shoulder of the dirt road. "We need to figure out where we are and where we need to go." He opened the door. "I'll climb a tree and see what I can see."

She craned her neck to look in the back seat of the SUV. "Maybe there is something in the vehicle that will be helpful, food or a flashlight."

"A flashlight would be good." He placed his feet on the packed earth and stared at the dark forest. Would he even be able to discern anything with only the moon and stars providing illumination? If there was a farm or any sort of occupied dwelling, he would see the glowing light even at a distance.

Quentin ambled toward the forest, choosing a tree that was tall and sturdy. As he gripped branches and pulled himself up, he could hear Willow rooting around and slamming doors.

He climbed high enough so he could see above the tree line. He was relieved to notice several clusters of nearby lights. He turned his head to the side where one of the lights started to flash and move.

It took him a moment to register that the moving

lights were a helicopter. Now he could hear the engine noises and the chopper headed in their direction.

Heart racing, adrenaline pumping, Quentin scrambled down the tree and ran toward the SUV where Willow was searching in the back. He touched her lightly. "We need to get out of here."

FIVE

The mechanical whir of the helicopter registered as Willow straightened and tilted her head toward the star-filled sky. One of the stars was moving.

She rushed around to the passenger side of the car while Quentin got behind the wheel. She hadn't even slammed the door when the car rolled forward.

Quentin didn't turn on the headlights. "I think our best hope is to hide." He veered off the road down a gradual embankment. He continued to drive in the dark, stopping when he came to some brush and rocks.

She peered out the back window at the approaching flashing lights. "We'll only remain hidden if he doesn't shine his light in this direction."

"I know," said Quentin. He pressed his head against the back of the seat.

Even with the windows rolled up, they could hear the helicopter.

Her heart still hadn't stopped racing from when Quentin had driven the car recklessly to get away from Yellowshirt. Almost crashing brought back memories of the accident. It had been raining the night Quentin drove down the winding mountain road. She, Luke and

Quentin had spent the day rock climbing and had mis-calculated how long it would take them to finish the climb and hike back to the car.

Willow pushed the memory aside only to be plunged into the danger of this present moment. Even though she slouched down in her seat, she could see the flashing lights through Quentin's window. The helicopter searched along the road. The guy on the ground must have a way to communicate with the man in the helicopter for him to locate her and Quentin so fast.

The helicopter remained close to the road, turning slightly one way and then the other. It pulled ahead of their hiding place and remained low to the ground.

The minutes ticked by as they waited for the flashing lights and noise of the blades to fade enough that it felt safe to move again. Willow craned her neck so she had a view of the chopper. When the lights disappeared, she took in a breath.

Quentin leaned forward and turned the key in the ignition. "He'll probably double back and search the road again when he doesn't find us. We're going to have to drive cross-country." Quentin didn't turn on the headlights.

"And hope we don't run out of gas."

The car rolled along the rough terrain. "I saw some lights not too far from here when I was up in the tree."

The car never got above fifteen miles an hour as he rolled over clumps of grass and low brush. Her breath caught when lights flashed in the rearview mirror. Sure enough, the chopper was headed back up the road looking for them.

The incline grew steeper and rockier. Quentin stopped the car and pushed open the door. She got out as well.

Her hope renewed when she saw the two lights in the distance ahead of them.

"The car won't make it down this hillside. We'll have to make a run for it."

As her eyes adjusted, she saw trees and rocks, some that were too big to navigate a car around and not enough space to get through.

He tugged on her sleeve.

They jogged through the darkness. The noise of the helicopter faded as they drew closer to the lights. Now she could see that the structure was a cabin porch light. The second light illuminated the yard. There was no garage, and she didn't see any cars.

They slowed down when they got to the edge of property. The cabin was completely dark.

"I don't think anyone is here," she said.

"It must be someone's vacation home or hunting cabin." Quentin stepped toward the porch.

As they drew closer, she saw that there was an alarm system set up on the house. "I left my cell phone in one of my camera bags. I don't suppose you have yours, do you? Maybe we're far enough down the mountain to get a signal."

Quentin touched his chest pocket. "I lost it somewhere." He studied the cabin again. "If we triggered that alarm system it might send someone up here to check it out."

She stared farther out hoping to see moving lights that would indicate a road connecting to more settlements. A few stationary lights glowed in the distance, probably farmhouses. "How long do you think it would take them to get up here?"

He took two more steps toward the cabin. "There might be a landline inside the cabin."

Breaking into any place felt wrong to her, but she realized they didn't have any other choice to save their lives. "We'll need to find out who the cabin belongs to and pay for any damages."

"Of course," said Quentin. He stepped up to the porch and took a moment to examine the alarm system. He tried the doorknob, which didn't budge. "I'm guessing it's the kind that is silent but sends a notice to law enforcement."

The noise of the helicopter growing louder made her heart pound. "Quentin, we need to hurry and get these lights turned off. He'll figure out this is where we went."

Quentin had already stepped across the porch and picked up a log. He broke one of the windows, undid the latch and pushed it open.

While Quentin crawled through the window, the helicopter drew closer. She sprinted up the porch steps. Both lights went out. She glanced over her shoulder, unable to discern if the helicopter was at the right angle to see that the lights had been turned off or to see them at all.

The door swung open and Quentin ushered her in. His hand brushed her back in a protective way, a familiar gesture that caused unbidden memories to surface. Until the accident, she had always felt safe with Quentin.

In the darkness, she could make out the outline of furniture, most of it covered with sheets.

"Get down below the window, Willow." Quentin was already crouching, moving around the room searching. Willow dropped to the floor and pushed her back up against the wall. She'd caught a glimpse of the approaching helicopter's flashing lights before she sat down.

Quentin crawled into the living room and then down a hallway. He returned moments later and sat beside her. "I can't find any landline."

As her eyes adjusted to the darkness, she saw that the cabin was one big room with a living room and kitchen. The hallway Quentin had gone down must lead to a bedroom.

"So what do you do now? Wait?"

Quentin shifted his weight and pulled his knees toward his chest. "We don't have a lot of choice. That alarm should send law enforcement to this cabin. They need to find us here."

Though she didn't vocalize the fear, she prayed the law showed up before the men in the helicopter did.

Quentin was well aware that with a cabin this far from town, law enforcement might not show up for hours. The police force in the nearest town probably consisted of only a few people. A call sent from an alarm company might not be the highest priority if other things needed to be dealt with first.

Silence descended between them like a heavy smothering blanket. This was the first extended time of quiet since Henry had been killed. How long before Willow started to ask questions again about why he'd come back here?

Their breathing seemed louder in the darkness. They sat with their backs to the wall only inches apart. He was aware of her every movement and sound of her taking in air. Memories of holding her in his arms, kissing her, swirled through his head. Though he could not find the words now, there would have to come a time when they spoke about losing Luke and the fallout from the tragedy. Maybe five years had given them both some perspective. Perhaps they could heal some wounds. He couldn't help but think that was why his work had brought him back here. God was in this somehow.

The noise of the helicopter remained steady through the broken window.

Willow turned and peered outside, still crouching and barely putting her eyes above the windowsill. "It looks like he's not getting any closer."

"He's still looking though."

She sat down. For a moment, their shoulders touched. She jerked away and then rested her back against the wall. Her response was almost involuntary. The gesture was enough to tell him that she still harbored anger toward him if she could not bear for them to be physically close.

He longed to find the words that might mend things between them. Though he prayed for guidance, no ideas came to him, and they sat in silence and waited.

"I left a lot of expensive camera gear on that helicopter," she said. "Wonder if I will get it back."

"Hard to say. If they fear being caught, they might try to escape in the chopper." He was grateful she at least wanted to fill the time with small talk.

She laced her fingers together. "We are not home safe yet, are we?"

"No…not yet." He could no longer hear the helicopter. His throat was parched, and his stomach growled. "I think it's safe for me to move around. You must be hungry and thirsty. I know I am."

She rested her head against the wall. "I could use a drink of water."

Quentin rose to his feet but made sure not to stand in front of the window where he might be visible. He walked to the kitchen area, opened a cupboard and felt around in the dark. Anything that mice might get into was probably not left behind, but maybe there were some canned goods. The cupboard was empty. When he tried the faucet on the kitchen sink, no water came out. It was probably connected to a generator that had been turned off.

He opened another cupboard door. His fingers touched some metal. He put the first can close to his eyes. Beans—and it would require finding a can opener. The second can was peaches with a pull top. The juice would at least hydrate them. He pulled out several more cans but none of them had a pull top. A quick search through a couple of drawers yielded a plastic spoon but no can opener.

He walked the short distance across the floor, allowing himself a quick glance through the window, where he saw no flashing lights in the air. Quentin sat down beside Willow and pulled the top off the can. "You can have the first sip."

"Thank you." She took a sip and handed the can back to him.

He drank the thick sweet liquid. Then he lifted the spoon. "Do you want any of the peaches?"

She took a couple of bites and then handed the can back to him. She wiggled. "My legs are getting cramped. I'm going to walk around. I'll stay away from the windows."

Quentin was glad she was aware of the need to be

cautious. He knew the chopper could have landed. The murderers might be approaching on foot to surprise them. Even with the lights off, the cabin might have been visible. They just couldn't take any chances.

He ate the rest of the peaches while she paced. She came and sat down beside him.

After several minutes passed, she spoke up. "Where have you been the last five years, Quentin? Did you even stay in touch with your dad?" Her voice was filled with accusation.

His stomach knotted. The taste of the peaches rose up his throat. She was trying a new tack with the same anger behind it. At least she wasn't asking him what he knew about those two men.

"I got word to my father that I was okay." He tried not to sound defensive, but her tone brought all the unresolved emotion to the surface. Her words *I don't love you anymore* echoed through his mind. "We should just let this go for now. I don't want to get into a fight."

She didn't answer right away. "Yeah, maybe we should."

Her words were like jabs to his heart. Thinking God had brought him back here for more than work had been a mistake.

Both of them jerked at the sound of car tires rolling over gravel. Quentin swung around. Still crouching, he peered above the windowsill.

"Can you tell who it is?"

The car had just turned into the dirt parking area by the cabin. The headlights remained on while a man got out and pulled a gun from a holster. Highway patrol. He had to have been alarmed by the broken window and assumed that the situation was dangerous.

Quentin needed to make himself known without being shot first. He could hear the lawman step onto the porch. Quentin ducked down out of sight and shouted, "Sir, please don't shoot. We're the ones who broke the window, but we're not criminals."

"I need you to come out with your hands up. Open the door slowly and step outside."

"Yes, sir." He leaned toward Willow. "Let me go out first."

Willow nodded. He brushed past her, standing up only when he was not in view of the window.

"I'm opening the door now," said Quentin. "I'm not armed."

"Step out real slow. Keep your hands where I can see them."

Quentin twisted the knob and pushed the door open. He stood on the threshold with his hands up. The lawman had moved back down to stand beside his vehicle. Quentin squinted as the headlights shone in his eyes. He could see the lawman only in silhouette.

"Is someone else in there with you?"

"Yes, a woman."

"Step to one side." The lawman twisted slightly sideways. "Ma'am?"

"Yes." Willow's voice sounded faint and afraid.

"I need you to come out same as your friend here. Hands in the air where I can see them."

"Okay." Quentin heard shuffling and footsteps. "I'm almost to the door."

Willow stepped outside.

The deputy spoke with a commanding voice. "I need the two of you to come down the stairs. I'm going to have to handcuff you and check you for weapons until I can clear that room."

"Sir, there were two men murdered up by Glacier Falls. We were pursued by the killers. They might still be up there." The lawman was following procedure, not taking any chances. But Quentin hoped he could hurry things along.

"That may be well and true. But the broken window and triggered alarm means a potential robbery."

"I used to be a deputy myself over in Little Horse. Quentin Decker."

"Don't know the name. Please put your hands behind your back." Quentin had to give the man credit. He was by the book.

Quentin decided the best thing would be to comply and then get more law enforcement up here as quickly as possible. The patrolman handcuffed Willow and Quentin and then entered the cabin with his weapon drawn.

Willow and Quentin stood beside the highway patrol car while the officer cleared the rest of the cabin.

"If we can get some police up here in a chopper maybe we can catch those guys before they get away," said Quentin.

"I have a feeling they will be long gone before that. I can identify both men. The guy in the yellow shirt wasn't very memorable, but I'll never forget the other guy's face, and he had a dragonfly tattoo on his chest."

All the air compressed out of Quentin's lungs, and he wheezed in a raspy breath. Mr. Smith had been on this mountain, and Willow had seen him. "Did he see you?"

"Just for a second. But his face is stuck in my head. I have a near photographic memory remember."

Mr. Smith knew he'd been spotted. That meant Willow had an even bigger target on her back.

SIX

Willow was grateful when the highway patrolman came back out of the cabin. Quentin's whole mood had shifted when she had said she'd seen both of the murderers. She thought she detected fear in his voice. Again, she was struck by the sense that he was hiding something from her.

The highway patrolman holstered his weapon but didn't move to uncuff either of them. "Now, why don't you two tell me what is going on? You say there was a murder up at Glacier Falls?"

Quentin relayed all that had taken place, ending with, "We need to get a helicopter up there quick."

"This county doesn't own a chopper. It will take at least a day to requisition one from another county," said the patrolman. "I will inform the sheriff of what you told me, and we'll get an investigation underway."

"We both would be glad to make statements about what happened," said Quentin.

"We'll pay for the damage to the cabin," said Willow.

The lawman crossed his arms. After a moment, he spoke up. "I believe you. I can take the cuffs off." He stepped toward them.

"If you could give us a ride back up the mountain, that'd be great. There are two vehicles parked at the trailhead that leads to Glacier Falls," Quentin said.

"Why don't I take you folks into town. I'm sure you're tired, and yes, we need to get statements from you both. I'll make arrangements for the vehicles to be brought down."

Willow rubbed her wrists after the lawman uncuffed her. "I have some expensive camera gear in the helicopter if it is found. My cell phone is in there too."

"If things are as bad as you say, the whole place will be a crime scene. Gonna take at least half a day to get the forensic team to come from one county over. I'll get your camera gear to you as quickly as possible."

They drove into the small town of Beaverhead, where the sheriff took their statements while the highway patrolman and a deputy headed up the mountain to get the vehicles and secure the area where the murders had taken place. Quentin gave them the keys to his car and described where the cars were, including the one they had taken from the thieves.

Willow wasn't sure what they would find. Had the men escaped in the helicopter or one of the cars? As she sat in the interview room reading over her statement, the only things she knew for sure were that she was exhausted, hungry and in need of a shower. Even if they did get her car back soon, she wasn't going to make the hundred-mile drive home without eating and resting. She signed her statement and pushed it across the table to the sheriff.

"This looks good," said the sheriff. Quentin had made his statement in a separate room.

Willow assumed that she was on her own at this

point. "Is there a place to grab some food and maybe a place to rest while I wait for my car?"

"There is a corner grocery store three blocks south and a motel just up the street from there. The motel is mostly used by hunters, so I am sure they have vacancies. Grocery store won't be open for a while, but the coffee shop across the street might have some sandwiches or pastries."

"Thank you."

When she stepped out of the interview room, Quentin was sitting flipping through a magazine as if he'd been waiting for her. "You going to get something to eat?"

"Yes," Willow said. Quentin seemed to assume they were going to stick together.

"I'll go with you. I'm hungry too."

Her chest felt like it was in a vise that was being tightened. The longer she was around him, the more she realized a lot of hurt and anger lay just beneath the surface. She'd kept it at bay for five years by staying busy with her job. Time did not heal all wounds, and the only thing that had made the pain bearable was geographic distance. "I can't stop you. It sounds like there's only one place that is open anyway."

He rose to his feet. "Great."

She stepped outside into the early morning light. Beaverhead had all of two stoplights. All the stores looked to be closed at this hour. They walked past a hardware store, a thrift store and the corner grocery. The coffee shop lights were on, and she could see a woman in a white apron.

They crossed the street. The bell above the door announced their entrance. Two teenagers sat sipping coffee from paper cups. The woman behind the counter ran a hand over her gray hair and smiled at them. "What can I do for you folks?"

The last thing Willow wanted was coffee. She stared at the display counter which was mostly pastries and cookies. "Do you have anything more substantial?"

"I can heat up a croissant with ham and cheese on it."

"That sounds great." Willow had gone so long without food her stomach no longer growled. It just ached.

Quentin stood close to Willow. "I'll have one too please."

"They're in the back. It'll just take me a second." The woman disappeared.

Willow turned slightly sideways. She could feel the teenagers staring at her and Quentin. In a town this small, strangers stuck out like a sore thumb. The microwave whirred in the back room.

"You want anything to drink?" Quentin pointed toward the bottles and cans on display. "Orange juice? Something without caffeine."

Once again, he seemed to be assuming they were going to eat together. "If it's all the same to you, I'm just going to take my food and go to the motel."

"Are you sure?" The comment didn't sound like he was hurt so much as afraid.

She touched her jacket pocket remembering that she'd left her wallet in the glove compartment of her car. "Actually, can you loan me some money? I left my wallet with my license and money in the car. I'll pay you back as soon as they get my car to me."

"Sure, but your sandwich will be cold by the time you get checked into your motel. Why don't we sit down and eat together?"

More than anything she wanted to quell the strong dark feelings that rose to the surface when she was close to Quentin. They weren't going to get anything resolved about the past. She feared they would just end up in an argument. He was right about her sandwich getting cold though. "Okay. But I'm too tired to talk. Can we just eat?"

"Sure."

The woman returned with sandwiches on paper plates. Quentin grabbed two orange juices and paid for their food. They chose a table opposite of where the teenagers, who were looking at their phones, sat.

The sandwich was warm and satisfying, and she tried to focus on that. She swallowed her last bite and took the final sip of orange juice. She pushed her chair back to leave.

Quentin reached across the table and put his hand on hers. "Willow, I am concerned about your safety. That those men will come after you since you saw both of them."

"How would they even find me? If they show up here because it's the closest town, they would be spotted right away."

"I just think maybe we should stay together."

She pulled her hand away. His touch could still make her feel weak in the knees. "The sheriff could protect me as well as you. When I get back to Little Horse, I'll let the police know what's going on. Honestly, Quentin, those men are probably halfway across the state by now. I'm sure they don't want to get caught." She stood up.

Quentin rose to his feet. "I just want you to be safe."

She shook her head. "There is something you're not telling me."

He pressed his lips together.

And he still wasn't going to tell her.

"I'm just very tired. I'm going to get some rest and go home as soon as I can." She pivoted and walked toward the door, but then she turned back around. "Sorry to do this, but can I borrow some money for the motel? I'm good for it."

He smiled. "I know you are, Willow."

She stepped outside. Up the street, she saw several more law enforcement cars parked by the sheriff's office. He must be getting help from neighboring towns. Hopefully, she'd be home before too long.

When she glanced back over her shoulder Quentin stood in the doorway. He smiled when she looked at him. Right now, she'd prefer that anyone but Quentin protect her.

Quentin's heart ached as he watched Willow make her way up the street to the motel. The chasm between them was just too deep. It seemed like even being close to him upset her. She had no idea how dangerous Mr. Smith was. Telling her would have meant blowing his cover.

He was glad to see there was more law enforcement in town. He ambled up the street back toward the hardware store which he hoped would open soon. He needed to get a new phone and call his handler to let him know what had happened. Willow had seen Mr. Smith. It might be that he could get permission to tell Willow what was going on and get her some protection. Maybe they would sit her down with a sketch artist. She was the first person to see Mr. Smith and live to tell about it.

When he walked past the hardware store, he saw

that it wouldn't open for another hour. The sheriff was standing outside the police station talking to another man in uniform. He decided to cross the street and find out what kind of progress they'd made.

The sheriff noticed him as he approached.

"Did your men make it up there?"

The sheriff nodded. "Pretty grim scene. I got a search and rescue crew coming to transport the bodies out. Forensics is headed up there in a few hours."

"What about the cars?"

"Around back. We located the chopper. It was almost out of fuel, otherwise I'm sure they would have used it to escape. We're trying to find a pilot to get it out of there," said the sheriff. "I'll show you where the cars are." The sheriff walked up an alley with Quentin beside him. The back of the sheriff's office featured a parking lot and an area surrounded by a chained-link fence that must function as a small impound yard. Within the fence were several cars and an ATV. The sheriff pointed to the corner where Quentin's car was parked. The car they had taken from the murderers was there as well. "Willow's car?"

"We figure that's how the two men got away."

Quentin's stomach clenched. That meant the murderers would find her wallet with the license in it. They'd know her name and address. He had to find a way to protect Willow. Quentin thanked the sheriff. "I'll be in town for at least a couple more hours. Willow is sleeping, and it looks like she might need a ride. Let me know of any more developments."

The sheriff touched his balding head. "You sure show a lot of curiosity for a civilian."

"Sorry, force of habit. I used to be a deputy about two counties over."

"But you're not anymore?"

Quentin shook his head. "Long time ago."

"We left the keys for your car in the glove compartment when you're ready to take it."

"Thanks." Quentin walked around to Main Street and crossed over to the hardware store. Still a while before it opened up. He paced. When the clerk saw him, he opened the door. "You look like you're waiting. You can come in early if you want."

Quentin stepped inside and looked around.

The clerk spoke to him as he was headed back toward the cash register. "Are you looking for something in particular?"

"Phone."

"We usually have a few of those in stock, but I sold out. Should be getting a shipment before the end of the week."

"Thanks anyway, but I need it sooner." He headed toward the door. Though he was sure the sheriff would allow him to use the landline in the office, he didn't want to risk being overheard. He'd have to delay calling his handler. Nothing to do now but wait for Willow to wake up, so he could let her know about her car and offer her a ride.

He stepped outside. He had a view of the motel down the street. Only one car was parked outside. If anyone pulled up, he'd be able to see it. He doubted the murderers would show up in the car they'd stolen. The biggest danger was that Willow's home address was on the license. For sure, he didn't want her returning home alone and maybe not at all given the level of risk.

He sat down on a bench, enjoying the warmth of the sun. He closed his eyes. As long as he kept moving, he hadn't been aware of how tired he was. But once he sat down, it hit him like a ton of bricks. He crossed his arms as he felt himself nodding off.

His head jerked, and his eyes opened.

A boy of about eight was sitting on the bench sipping from a plastic cup and watching him.

"Whoa, guess I fell asleep."

The kid rubbed his freckled cheek and swung his legs back and forth. "You sure did, mister."

The bank clock across the street indicated that he'd been asleep for at least twenty minutes. The boy had hair so red it was orange in the sunlight. "Did I snore?"

The kid sipped his drink. "If you got to sleep, you got to sleep."

"So true." The kid's reaction made him smile. He had always liked kids. When he and Willow had been engaged and making plans for their future, they had talked about having a big family. Almost involuntarily, his hand went over his heart. Thinking about the past and what might have been was counterproductive.

A woman holding a younger girl's hand came around the corner and up the street. The redheaded kid waved at them. He looked at Quentin. "Nice talkin' to ya." He burst up from the bench and ran to meet his mom and sister.

Quentin chuckled as the kid hurried away with his family. When he drew his attention back to the motel where Willow was sleeping, he noticed a truck parked on the other side of the first smaller compact that had been there before he fell asleep. He surveyed the streets, not seeing any other new cars.

He couldn't take any chances. He headed toward the motel. The smart thing to do would be to take measures as quickly as possible to get Willow to a protected place. Convincing her of that would be a challenge.

SEVEN

Willow woke from a deep sleep to the sound of someone knocking on her door. At first, it didn't register with her, and then fear set in. Her heart skipped into overdrive.

She was still on her guard from all that had happened. She was still half asleep and not ready yet to get up and peer through the peep hole.

Quentin's voice was muffled by the door. "Willow, it's me. I am so sorry to wake you, but we need to talk."

The only way she could not be stirred up about the past was to not be around Quentin. Why was he making this so hard? "I told you I would inform the police what happened when I get back to Little Horse."

"The murderers took your car. That means they probably found your license and know where you live."

Still half asleep she couldn't fully process what he had said. She pulled back the blanket and placed her feet on the floor. "Are you saying they will come after me?" As the information sunk in, terror invaded her awareness. They knew who she was and where she lived.

"Probably, I can give you a ride back to Little Horse

and take you directly to the police station. Please, Willow, this is serious."

She got up, crossed the room and drew back the dead bolt. When she opened the door, she could read the tension in the way his lips formed a straight line and his eyebrows drew together. His expression softened when he saw her. His blue eyes brightened. "Thank you for opening the door."

"I don't have a lot of choice here, do I?"

"The sheriff is pretty busy dealing with the crime scene so he can't take you."

"Come inside. I need to clean up a little. I crashed as soon as I got into the room."

He nodded and stepped across the threshold as she made her way to the bathroom. After washing her hands, Willow splashed some water on her face. "Do you know if the sheriff brought my camera gear down?" She reached for a towel and dried her face.

"They're trying to find someone who can pilot the helicopter."

She needed that equipment. She grabbed a washcloth and ran it under the warm water which felt soothing in her hands. While she wiped down her neck, she caught a glimpse of herself in the mirror. Her blond hair had come loose of the French braid she kept it in. She had a scratch on her cheek.

She stepped back into the room. Quentin sat in a chair by the window. The sun shining through the window created a sort of halo effect around his head and brought out the golden highlights in his hair. He had always shaved just enough to keep a five o'clock shadow visible. He was just as handsome as he had been five years ago.

It would take an hour and a half to get home. It would be the longest ninety minutes of her life.

"My car is just across the street behind the sheriff's office." He rose to his feet.

Dread knotted her stomach. What were they even going to talk about without getting into a fight?

After leaving the room key on the bureau, she stepped outside. He followed, closing the door behind him.

There were several more police vehicles parked outside the sheriff's office than when she had checked into the motel. Quentin led her around the back to where his car was parked. They both got in.

Quentin started the engine. "You want to get some coffee for the road?"

"I think I'd rather try to sleep. I got less than an hour's rest." The power nap had actually revived her, but closing her eyes would be the excuse she needed to not engage in conversation with Quentin.

"I'm pretty tired. I'm going to need coffee in a bit." Quentin drew his attention to the coffee shop across the street where they had gotten the sandwich. Through the glass windows he could see there was a line of people. "Looks like there is quite a wait."

"There's a drive-through kiosk in that little whistle stop up the road about ten miles," Willow said.

"Is that still in business?"

"Yes, it's still there." Her tone held a snippy quality she hadn't intended. Even small talk reminded her of the history between them. It was only a little over an hour and then she wouldn't have to deal with the strong feelings being around Quentin caused.

A silent tension entered the car as Quentin backed up, pulled out of the lot and rolled toward the street.

As he reached the town limits, she closed her eyes but realized she wasn't going to be able to sleep. She kept her eyes closed anyway.

"Mind if I put on the radio? You know I've always had a hard time with silence."

"No, go ahead."

Quentin found a station that played classical music, something he'd always liked. One of the things that she had loved about Quentin was that he was cultured and well-read. One of her favorite things they did together was to spend afternoons sitting on the couch, each reading the same classic book and then talking about it.

She opened her eyes as the forested landscape and farmland clicked by. She hadn't dated anyone since Quentin left town. She hadn't wanted to.

They came to the little town that had the drive-through kiosk. The town itself was less than five hundred people, consisting of a post office, a farm supply store, grain silos and a few homes.

Quentin slowed as he entered the small town. "Are you sure you don't want anything?"

"I guess I could use a latte."

"With a shot of vanilla, right?"

"Thanks for remembering."

"There's a lot I remember, Willow." His voice held a warm quality.

Her heart fluttered, and she was able to think of the love they'd shared, not what had torn them apart.

Quentin pulled up to the kiosk, opened his window and turned down the volume on the radio. He spoke to the young woman in the kiosk when she slid her window open. "Mocha, the medium size and a small latte with a shot of vanilla."

The woman took Quentin's money and closed the window while she prepared the drinks.

The music played low, and the car engine hummed while they waited. Willow focused on the beauty of the violin music spilling out of the car speakers.

The woman slid open the window and handed the drinks to Quentin. He turned the radio back up, set his coffee in the holder and pulled back out onto the road.

The remainder of the trip was mostly silent, and they exchanged the barest of words about the traffic and the road they were on.

They passed the sign that read Welcome to Little Horse. Quentin clicked the blinker and got into the lane to make one of the city's two exits. Little Horse had a population of twenty thousand. While still mostly an agricultural town that was supported by its proximity to Yellowstone National Park, the town was growing.

"Who is the city police chief these days?" Quentin drove through a shopping district, past signs that indicated where the community college, museum and hospital were.

"No one you would know. He's a transplant from Chicago. His last name is Craig. I don't remember his first name."

"I wonder if anyone on the force is someone I would know. The sheriff's office coordinated with the city quite a bit. I knew most of the guys."

"I have no idea. I'm out of town a lot with work. Really haven't kept up with that."

He turned down several streets until they were in

front of the police station. "I'll go inside and explain the situation. You should come with me."

"I'd rather wait in the car." While she appreciated that he was probably being protective, she needed some space from him.

Quentin shrugged. "Guess it's pretty safe by a police station."

She watched as Quentin walked up the steps of the city police station. She looked to one side and then the other. A car eased by behind her. She glanced in the rearview mirror. The silver car looked nothing like hers. Aware of how vulnerable she was alone in the car, she reached over to driver's side and clicked the buttons that locked all the doors. Maybe she should have gone inside with him.

Though she suspected that if the men did come after her like Quentin said they would, they would ditch her car. It would be too easy to be caught in a car that had been reported as stolen.

Quentin returned moments later. She unlocked all the doors so he could get behind the wheel. "I explained the situation. They will send a guy out to do a patrol of your place, but they can't give better protection for most of the day. They just don't have the manpower. There's a big football game this weekend so lots of shenanigans and intoxicated people. It's going to keep them pretty busy. Right now, they are all down on Main Street putting up barriers for the parade."

"So what do we do?"

"I don't think it's a good idea for you to be at your place. I need to stop somewhere to get a phone for starters. I have an important call to make. I can stay with you for a bit until we can figure something out. Is there anyone who can come be with you?"

"Just my mom."

"No, I mean someone who could protect you."

In the time since Quentin had left, most of her friendships had transformed into acquaintances. Really, Luke and Quentin had been her support and her deepest friendships. She'd become pretty self-reliant since then. The realization stung. "Maybe one of the guys from church." She couldn't think of anyone. Though she still went on Sunday mornings when she was in town, she hadn't maintained relationships from the small group Bible study that she and Quentin had attended together. The accident, Luke's death and Quentin leaving had ripped her world to pieces.

"Really? Who?" His level of curiosity had intensified.

She stared out the window at the city passing by. "No one, Quentin. There has been no one since you."

"That's not what I was implying." A defensive tone colored his words.

She let out a heavy breath and shook her head. Being around him was so hard.

He drove for a few minutes more until he entered the parking lot by a store that sold electronics. After turning off the engine and pulling the key out, he looked at her. "For your own safety, I'll stay with you until I can find someone. Maybe there is a friend in the sheriff's department who can help. I know you don't like being around me."

"How do you know how much danger I'm in?" She let her words fall like rain knowing he wouldn't tell her what was really going on.

Quentin stared through the windshield. His jawline hardened. "I need to get a phone. What are you going to do until you get your phone back? I can get you one too."

She didn't want to be any more in debt to Quentin than she already was. "I have a thing set up so I can check messages on my phone remotely. Maybe before the day is over I'll get it back, along with my camera gear."

"You're welcome to use my phone."

"I can wait a little while." A lot of those jobs would go to another photographer if her response wasn't quick. Up until now, she hadn't thought about the loss of income this would cause. Maybe she would have to rethink his offer.

"I'll be right back." He pushed open the door and headed toward the store.

Willow sat with her arms crossed as she watched Quentin open the door of the store and disappear inside. Her throat grew tight, like she might cry. She lifted her chin; she pressed her lips together. No way was she going to shed tears over all this turbulent emotion.

A car rolled into the parking lot. She glanced in that direction and then did a double take. It was the same car that had been at the police station. The driver was not either of the two men who had been at the falls. He turned and looked at her, offering a wide grin and a row of metal teeth.

Something about the way he stared made alarm bells go off. She was grateful to see that a truck had just parked several spaces down. Two burly-looking men got out and headed toward the store. If the guy in the car was up to something, he wouldn't try anything with people around.

Heart racing, she pushed open the door. Trailing behind the two bulky men, she hurried inside to find Quentin.

Quentin drew his attention away from the display of phones to see Willow coming toward him up the aisle. He knew her well enough to understand what that expression meant. Her face blanched, and her full lips pressed together so tightly they formed a thin line. Something had frightened her.

He reached out to her as she drew close. She was visibly shaking. His hand rested on her upper arm. "Everything okay?"

"There was a man in the parking lot. He was at the police station too, same car."

"Was it one of the men who—"

She shook her head. "He had teeth, metal teeth."

Quentin hurried to the front of the store and looked out the large display windows. His car was the only one parked there. Maybe it was just a coincidence, but he couldn't treat it like one if he was going to keep Willow safe. How had they been found so quickly and another man dispatched? He wondered if the two murderers had left a tracking device on his car.

Willow came up behind him. He turned to face her. "Let's get this phone and go. I don't think you should go back to your house just yet." They could be waiting there for her.

She gazed up at him and nodded. "Okay, I'll do what you say." Her words were soft and filled with trust.

She hadn't put up any protest to his suggestion. Progress…maybe? Didn't she remember the man he'd been when they were together? He would have taken a bullet for her…still would.

Maybe she finally understood the level of danger she was in. Quentin returned to the aisle where the phones were displayed and grabbed one. He paid for it, and he and Willow headed back to his car. Once she was seated inside, he did a cursory look underneath the car for a tracking device but found nothing.

He sat behind the wheel and handed her the phone. "Can you activate that for me?"

"Sure." She took the phone and started to try to get the packaging open. He handed her his pocketknife. "Thanks."

He wasn't sure where they should go. Someplace public where Willow wasn't likely to be harmed but a place where he could make a phone call to his handler and not risk being overheard. He thought of his dad on the ranch outside town.

His communication with his father over the last five years had been just enough to let his dad know he was okay. When he knew his work would bring him close to Little Horse, he'd called his father to let him know he'd try to swing in for a visit but couldn't tell him when and couldn't commit to it for sure. His work required that he be ready to fly across the globe at a moment's notice if the trail went hot for catching anyone connected to the smuggling ring.

Willow cut through the plastic packaging and pulled out the phone.

He started the car, backed up and pulled out onto the street. They passed the high school where he and Willow had met. She was a freshman when he was a junior. Willow had just moved here with her mother and Luke after her father's death. He remembered a bright-eyed blonde challenging him to a game of what she called "killer badminton" in gym class. He smiled at the memory.

Willow, her attention on the phone, didn't notice they were driving past the high school.

Sadness washed over him. Maybe they couldn't repair the chasm between them, but he had to make sure she was safe from Mr. Smith and his goons. He remembered a park not too far from the high school that might provide a private place to make his phone call.

He wove through the streets.

Willow looked up just as the phone made a beeping noise. "Where are you going?"

"I'm trying to find that park we used to hang out at on our lunch breaks."

"You're on the wrong street. Take a left up here."

"There are a lot of new buildings around here. Didn't this used to be an open field?"

"Five years is a long time, Quentin," Willow said. "Things change." Again, the bitterness had seeped into her words.

No matter how careful they both tried to be about conversational topics, it always seemed to veer back to the pain they'd caused each other. He chose not to react. If he could keep control of his feelings maybe that would be the start of them being able to talk. "So where is the park?"

She stared through the windshield. "Take a right on Hanson Street. You'll see it in about three blocks."

"Okay, some of this is starting to look familiar," Quentin said.

She stared back down at the phone. "I think this phone is ready to go."

He pulled into a parking space. This time of day the park wasn't too busy. Mostly moms with young children. There was a playground, a picnic area and a climbing wall. The climbing wall was new.

Willow handed him the phone. "I'm going to stretch my legs. I won't go far."

He nodded and got out. The number to get in touch with his handler was not in any phone, only in his head. He stepped out of earshot of Willow, who walked with her arms crossed and her head down.

He stared at the phone, pressed in the number and looked up. Willow sprinted toward him, fear etched across his face.

"That's him. That's the car that was at the hardware store." She pointed to where a car had parked across the street, not in the lot for the park.

"Are you sure?"

The car door opened, and a man got out. He stalked toward the park. The bulk underneath his jacket meant he was armed. Then his gaze rested on Willow, and his hand moved toward where the gun was.

Without a gun, Quentin had no way to defend them but to flee. Standing a foot away from him, Willow seemed almost frozen with fear.

He grabbed her sleeve and pulled her toward the car hoping to shake her free of the paralysis of terror. "Get to the car now, Willow. Run."

EIGHT

Willow sprinted the short distance to the car, flung open the door and got in. Quentin had already slipped behind the wheel and turned the key in the ignition.

As Quentin shifted into Reverse and hit the gas, she could see through the side window the man running back to his car. She had just seen him reach for what was probably a gun when Quentin had commanded her to get to the car.

The tires squealed on pavement as he pulled out onto the road and headed toward Main Street.

Willow noticed the increase in the amount of people parked on the side street. "Quentin, the parade, the barriers. We won't be able to cross Main Street."

"Forgot." He jerked the wheel. He rumbled down an alley and found a parking space on the backside of a cluster of boutique stores.

She peered down the alley just in time to see the silver car rolling by slowly enough to indicate he might have spotted them but not in time to make the turn. It would be only a matter of minutes before he circled the block and came up the other way. Though there were plenty of cars, she saw no other people. Most of the town was probably on Main Street watching the parade.

"It would be best if we didn't just sit here. He's not likely to try to harm us or even be able find us in the crowd," Quentin said as he opened the door. "Stay close to me."

She couldn't argue with him. A car rolled through the alley looking for an elusive place to park. Traffic was still jammed out on the street and would be at a standstill until the parade was over. Trying to go the other way back to where they had been would be a challenge.

After she got out of the car, they walked the half block up the alley. They were two blocks from Main, and the streets were teeming with people trying to get a good position to see the parade.

Her heart pounded as she glanced around. Quentin eased in beside her.

A man bumped into her, and she nearly fell backward. Quentin caught her, wrapping his arm across her back.

"Oh sorry, miss." From the smell of the man's breath, he'd been drinking.

Quentin guided her toward a brick building a block from Main. She could hear the marching band coming up the street.

"Put your back against the wall and face outward so you have the max amount of view of what is around you," said Quentin.

The crowd cheered and clapped. She could only guess at what float had caused such an outburst. The float with the team on it was usually one of the last ones and got the strongest response.

She stared out at the crowd milling around, cringing every time she spotted someone who resembled the man with the metal teeth.

Quentin leaned close, his shoulder pressed against hers. While everyone else's focus was on trying to see what was going down Main Street, they watched the crowd. The cheers of children rose up.

"I've missed all the Little Horse traditions," Quentin said, leaning close and whispering in her ear. "I've missed this town."

Willow watched a family go by on the street. A father carrying one child and the other in a stroller. Both kids had balloons. Somehow, she couldn't help but think this should be her life by now. Married with kids and enjoying the traditions of a small town.

Her spine stiffened when she thought she saw the man with the metal teeth not more than ten feet away. Sensing he was being watched, the man looked in her direction. It wasn't him. She let out a breath.

They waited until the noise of the parade faded and the crowds started to disperse.

"Let's get to the car now."

"We won't be able to beat the traffic. We'll just get caught up in it."

"There's a degree of safety in the crowd."

They pushed through the throng of people. Quentin remained close. Though his touch still caused her heart to beat faster, she didn't mind him placing his arm across her back in a protective way.

At the car, Quentin waited with the engine running while other cars were pulling out. When most of the vehicles in the alley were gone, he backed out and eased into traffic on the crowded street. Traffic was bumper-to-bumper and moving slowly.

Quentin surged forward just as a man stepped out into the street. The man pounded the hood and gave Quentin a crude gesture. His face was contorted with anger.

The noise made Willow's breath catch. She was still on high alert.

Quentin shook his head. "That guy came out of nowhere." The cars had stopped completely. Quentin reached over and patted Willow's arm. "You okay?"

"I'll survive." Her heart was still racing. "We need a plan. The police really can't help?"

"Not until the game is over. I'm sure it's the same story at the sheriff's office. Lots of drinking, lots of fights, lots of traffic stops."

He eased the car forward.

She looked side to side and then out the back window.

"If we can get through town, we can go out to my dad's place until this blows over. It's quiet there, if you don't mind hanging out with me for a while longer."

"I really just want to go home."

"Willow, they know your address."

"Can we at least go there, and I can get a few things and grab the money I owe you?"

Quentin seemed to be contemplating her request as the rolled a few feet. "What would you say is the safety level? How close are your neighbors?"

"I have neighbors across the street and on one side of me."

"Okay, we'll go there and then out to my dad's place. What street is it?"

"221 J Street. It runs east to west." What Willow wanted more than anything was to turn back time by two days. To never have taken the Vertical Limit job or to have seen Quentin again. To be in her own safe, warm house packing for some job thousands of miles from here.

"I think I remember how to get there."

Traffic started to thin out, and Quentin was able to go the speed limit. He wove through the streets until he arrived on J Street. He came to a stop on the street by her house.

She looked at her little house with the white fence and tulips blooming as if she was seeing it for the first time. She stared at the paving stones she'd put in herself that led up to the stairs and the door knocker she'd gotten at an antiques store. She wasn't the same person who had left here yesterday morning.

"You can pull in around the side. There's a concrete slab to park on."

Once the car was stopped, Quentin turned to face her. "You need to stay close to me, and you need to let me clear each room before you enter it."

"I just want to get some clothes and toiletries."

He looked off to the side. "That open field concerns me."

"Why?" Though she had no idea what he'd been doing in the years since he left, Quentin was a trained officer. She was sure he took note of every potential threat.

"Never mind. Let's get this done quickly." Quentin got out of the car.

She followed behind him as he checked the outside of the house, keenly aware that her home was no longer a safe place.

With Willow close behind him Quentin moved around the perimeter of the house. Satisfied that no one was hiding in the yard, they went to the front door after Willow retrieved a spare key she kept in a flower pot covered in rocks. "Were your house keys in the car that got stolen?"

"I can't remember if I put them in my camera gear or left them in the car."

So the thieves might have a key to her house. Though he didn't want to make Willow more fearful than she already was, the unkempt field by her house provided too many places for someone to hide. The brush was thick and high, and it looked like someone had treated it like a dump, leaving a rusting car body and other refuse.

Willow pushed open the door. He stepped inside, then checked behind furniture as well as looked out each window. She followed him as he cleared the kitchen and the main floor powder room. The house reflected Willow's taste. What had she called her style? Shabby chic. Lots of floral prints and stuff she bought and fixed up. The whole place was bright and welcoming.

He pointed at the stairs.

"My bedroom, office and bathroom are up there."

Quentin stepped ahead of her up the narrow stairway. The house must be from the early 1900s, though the kitchen looked updated. He pulled back the shower curtain that surrounded the claw-foot tub and cleared the rest of the bathroom. And then he moved toward her office. Framed photos hung on the wall and were stacked on the floor. Most of them must have been taken for her job. She even had some framed magazine covers as well as a stack of magazines by her computer that must feature her photos. Most of them were extreme sports or nature magazines. The photo of a grizzly bear looking directly at the camera sent a chill down his spine.

His eyes were drawn to the photos on a shelf above her desk. Pictures of him, Luke and Willow at the base of a ski hill, the three of them sitting at a restaurant and standing at a trailhead with their arms around each other. Sorrow washed over him and through him.

The floorboards creaked as Willow stepped into the office.

He pointed to the photos. "Feels like a lifetime ago."

"It was." Her voice faltered.

"I think about him almost every day."

She stepped a little closer toward the shelf and reached out for a photo. "Me too." She gazed at the image as her fingers touched Luke's face.

He brushed his hand over her back as she returned the photo to its place on the shelf. She didn't recoil from his touch. She turned and tilted her head. Wide brown eyes searched his. "We can at least agree that we had that in common."

"We both loved Luke?"

She nodded.

The exchange felt like progress to him. She hadn't gotten angry, and he didn't feel that tangled emotion he couldn't even name.

She stepped back, breaking the sacredness of the moment. "I just need to get a few things out of my bathroom and bedroom."

"The bathroom is clear. I'll go clear the bedroom."

He entered her bedroom which faced the open field. He checked her closet and under the bed. He could hear her moving around in the bathroom. The whole upstairs couldn't be more than eight hundred square feet. Willow came into the bedroom carrying a small makeup bag. She pulled out a backpack from the closet. "This is all packed. It's my go bag if I need to leave quickly for an assignment." She unzipped a pocket on the backpack and stowed the makeup case.

He stepped toward the window and drew back the curtain. On the far side of the field the sun caused a glint of metal. Someone had parked a car there. The brush made it impossible to tell what model it was. "Do you have some binoculars?"

She walked across the room, retrieved a case down from the closet shelf and handed it to him. He pulled out the binoculars. Panning slowly across the field, taking time to study the thicker brush and rusted car body, he didn't see any sign of movement.

"One second, I forgot something in the bathroom." She left the room.

He took another look at the field by her house with the binoculars. Still not seeing anything that alarmed him.

Something glass broke in the bathroom, and he heard Willow gasp.

NINE

Willow stepped back from the window, accidentally knocking a glass dish off the vanity by the sink. The silver car had just come up the street.

Quentin was at the door within seconds. "What is it?"

She tilted her head toward the window. "He's here."

Quentin eased toward the window, being careful to stay out of view. "He's not getting out. Several of your neighbors are in their front yards. He probably doesn't want to be identified."

"You mean since he intends to come in here and shoot us?"

"Two kids playing basketball are now staring at his car," Quentin said.

"Someone lingering on a dead-end street without getting out looks suspicious. Those two boys are really good kids, observant too," she said.

"He's leaving."

"Maybe he didn't realize it was a dead-end street."

"Who knows? We need to get out of here."

"He's just waiting for us at the corner," Willow said unable to keep the fear from making her voice falter.

"We can't stay here, Willow."

They clattered down the stairs. Willow grabbed the spare key on the entry table where she'd left it and made sure the door was locked. Ken and Andy, the brothers across the street, waved at her when she stepped outside.

"Get in the car. There is something I need to do before we go."

"What?"

"There has got to be a tracking device on my car, and I need to do a more thorough search. That guy may have been given your address, but he found us as soon as we were in town. I don't want to risk being tracked to the ranch."

She pointed up the street. "He'll probably just follow us there."

"I can shake him if I have to."

Ken and Andy stopped playing ball and went into their house. The street was quiet. She glanced to where the silver car had gone but couldn't see it. This end of J Street had only four houses on each side before it connected with the cross street.

Willow put her backpack in the back seat and got in the passenger seat. Quentin walked around the car, ducked down and disappeared. He must be looking under the car again.

She stared up the street again, and her heart beat a little faster.

Quentin opened the driver's side door but didn't get in. Instead, he pressed the hood release. He flipped up the hood. She could see nothing through the windshield.

The hood came back down. Quentin wiggled his hand, holding a small round device which he tossed toward the open field. He got in, turned around and sped up the street.

She kept checking the rearview mirror, half expecting to see the silver car. Quentin took a serpentine pattern through town. Little Horse appeared virtually abandoned. Not much traffic at all. Most people were on their way to the game.

Quentin's roundabout route meant they would avoid the traffic headed toward the fieldhouse where the game would happen in a few hours. The tailgating was probably already well underway.

Quentin drove to the edge of town and out onto the road to his family's ranch. Over the years she'd seen Quentin's dad around. Quentin had been the youngest of three boys and a late-in-life baby. When she'd asked Quentin's dad about him, his response had always been vague and general.

"Did you visit your father in the hospital when he had his heart attack?"

"Yes, Darren got in touch with me and I flew in."

Darren was Quentin's older brother. It sounded like Quentin had communicated with family members when needed. Did she mean so little to him that he couldn't even let her know he was alive?

"I figured my dad would let you know I was okay."

Was she that transparent that he could read what she was thinking? "You couldn't send me a postcard or a quick text?"

Quentin tapped his fingers on the steering wheel. "I wasn't sure if you even cared. What you said to me the last time I saw you was pretty final. That you didn't love me anymore."

She stared out the window as they passed open fields,

silos and farmhouses set back from the road. When she'd shouted that at him five years ago, had she really meant it, or was she just speaking out of her pain? What he told her helped her see the events from his point of view. "I'm sorry. That was a mean thing to say."

"Those words kind of drove me away."

Though he was a man in control of his emotions, she could detect the anger in his words.

His remark caused her to tense up. She had spent the years seeing things only from her point of view.

Quentin brought his car to a stop in front of the ranch house, a modular home with a wraparound porch. "My dad's truck isn't here."

"Would he have gone to the game?"

"If he was invited, I suppose he might go. Dad was never too big on the games unless I was playing."

"Does he have a cell phone you could call or text?"

Quentin let out a short laugh. "Dad is so not a tech guy. He still just has the landline."

"Maybe he just took his truck out in the field to check cattle or repair a fence."

"Maybe." Quentin shifted his weight in the seat and unclicked his seat belt. "Let me clear the perimeter real quick. I could look for dad's truck at the same time. If you could wait in the car with the doors locked, then we'll go into the house together."

She did as she was told. Quentin walked as though he was going to go around the house then stopped, thought better of it and went inside.

Willow sat up a little straighter. What was he doing? She locked the doors. Quentin emerged a moment later holding a gun which he placed in his waistband.

He disappeared around the side of the house. Next

to the house was a corral with two horses and the barn where she and Quentin had shared their first kiss when she was sixteen.

Maybe it was the confinement of the car or being in a place that was stirring up memories that she'd managed to bury, but she felt claustrophobic. Willow started to hyperventilate. She leaned over and placed her head between her knees.

This hadn't happened since after the car accident. She could hear Quentin pounding on the window and calling her name, but he seemed very far away. The sensation of hurling down a dark tunnel consumed her. The memory of Luke's screams as the car rolled down the mountainside pounded on her eardrums as though they were happening all over again. Her breath was shallow, and her heart raced. A blackness like blinders being pulled around her eyes surrounded her as noises from the crash replayed in her mind at a loud volume.

She heard a clicking noise and then Quentin gathered her into his arms. "It's all right. I got you." He must have found a way to trip the car door locks from outside.

She was shaking as he held her while she sat in the car seat.

"You okay to go inside?" His voice was gentle and filled with compassion.

She nodded.

He still supported her with his arms while she got out of the car and they headed up to the porch.

He drew her into a hug. She rested her head against his chest. Gradually, her heartbeat slowed and she could get her breath. He guided her inside and helped her sit down in a soft chair in the living room. He grabbed a throw and placed it over her. She tucked her legs up under her and rested her cheek against the chair.

Quentin wandered through the house. It sounded like he was checking all the doors and windows to make sure they were locked. She closed her eyes and rested. Quentin fussed around in the kitchen and then grew silent. All the talk about the past had stirred up the memory of the accident.

She fell into an even deeper dreamless sleep.

Sometime later, she felt his touch on her cheek. "Willow, wake up. I made you a grilled cheese and tomato soup."

She opened her eyes. She pulled the throw down off her shoulders. "How long was I out for?"

"Couple hours. I took a power nap myself. Are you up to sitting at the kitchen table?"

She nodded and placed her feet on the carpet. They settled at the kitchen table. Quentin put a steaming bowl of soup in front of her along with a sandwich on a plate. He got the same for himself and then sat opposite her.

She took several spoonfuls of the warm comfort food. And then a bite of the sandwich which tasted wonderful. Quentin had toasted the bread with butter and just a sprinkle of salt. "This is very good. Brings back memories. Riding horses out in the rain and coming in to have this to eat."

"I remember," he said. "I only had one specialty. You were always the best cook."

"It was a lifetime ago. We can't ever get back to the innocence, can we?"

He shook his head. "But maybe we can move on and heal."

It was good for them to be able to talk in a calm voice

about the past. It had been Quentin's kindness in making the soup and sandwich that reminded her of his good qualities and made her feel safe. "Maybe. I don't know." She gazed around the kitchen. Quentin had taken his gun out of his waistband and left it within reach on the counter. She shuddered when she saw it.

He held his spoon midair. Quentin had always been super tuned in to her emotional states. "You okay?"

The feeling of hurling down a dark tunnel returned, but this time she was able to right herself by focusing on Quentin. Looking into his blue eyes steadied her.

"Sorry for my meltdown earlier."

He shrugged. "I'm surprised it took as long as it did. You've been through a lot."

She glanced at the gun again. "I think it was everything. Seeing the gun. Being confined in the car. I started to remember the crash. The noises."

He reached across the table and rested his hand on hers. "The violence you've experienced triggered the trauma of the crash. I understand."

"I don't get it. I was fine until you came back." His hand still rested on hers. Her voice faltered, but the anger she had experienced when she first saw him was gone. "Why come back now? What is going on?"

"I hope I can answer that question for you. I have a really important phone call to make. If you're okay, I'll go on the porch for some privacy."

She was rested, and her belly was full. "I'll be fine."

He squeezed her hand before pulling away, offering her a quick smile. Quentin grabbed the cell phone he'd bought and stepped out on the porch. Willow finished the last of her meal and returned to the comfortable chair. The landline telephone was across the room.

She could check the messages that had come to her cell phone and call the sheriff to see if she could get her camera and gear back. She was anxious to return to her life and her work.

After gathering the throw around her, she decided to rest and then make the call in a few minutes. Outside, she could hear Quentin talking on his phone in a low voice, but with the windows closed, she could not discern any of the words.

She wondered who he was talking to and if his phone call would change anything.

Quentin dialed the memorized number of his handler, Joseph, and summarized all that had happened.

Joseph allowed a moment of silence before answering. "We heard some chatter about Henry being shot and that poor pilot."

"It was pretty awful. I have the feeling Henry would have opened up to me."

"Do you know if the necklace was found by Mr. Smith or the other guy?"

"I have no idea." Quentin turned and looked out at the horse corral. Beyond that, several Angus cows grazed. The rest of the herd must be up in the foothills. "My gravest concern right now is for Willow Farris. We know what Mr. Smith is capable of. She needs protection."

"You say you don't think your cover was blown?"

Quentin gripped the phone a little tighter. He felt like Joseph was focused on the case and not hearing what he was saying about his concern for Willow. "No, I don't think my cover was blown. I'm sure that Mr. Smith has done his research and found out I am from around here. It makes sense that I would be a guide for Vertical Limit."

"I am going to have to talk to my supervisor and figure out how we proceed. Obviously, we need to bring Miss Farris in and have her give a description to a sketch artist. We may be able to coordinate that through an FBI field office since we've been working jointly with them on this case."

Because the case was complex and international, other agencies, like US Customs, had been involved as well.

"What about protection for her?" Quentin rested his free hand on the porch railing. "Look, Willow and I have a romantic history together. It would feel a lot better to me if I could tell her that I am working undercover. She knows something is up. She won't be one to talk."

"I need to get clearance for that before I can give you permission. She'll have to be brought in for questioning anyway." Joseph spoke slowly as though he were mulling over options and trying to come up with the best way to proceed.

"My biggest concern right now is that Willow be safe," Quentin said.

Joseph continued as though he hadn't heard what Quentin said. "We know that Mr. Smith doesn't have a record. But maybe he made an appearance at some of the other Vertical Limit shoots or on a security camera when items were stolen. If she could put a sketch together for us, we might be able to use facial recognition software to see if he pops up anywhere."

"It needs to be sooner rather than later. We were followed through town. It's just a matter of time before Mr. Smith's henchman catches up with us."

"Let me make some phone calls. I can get back to you within the hour, and we'll figure out how to proceed. Are you in a safe place now?"

Quentin stared out at the road that led back into town then off toward the foothills and surrounding mountains. The nearest neighbor was five miles away. "Relatively."

"I'll call you back as soon as I know something."

"Okay, thank you." Quentin stepped inside where Willow had picked up his father's landline. She wasn't saying anything. She must be listening to her messages. She had gotten a piece of paper and was writing down something.

Willow hung up the phone. "I called the sheriff and then I called my phone to get my messages. They should be able to release my camera gear to me by the end of the day. They still haven't found my car." She looked at the piece of paper. "I had some calls for possible jobs. I need to get back to work."

"I'm not sure you will be able to do that just yet. Were there any messages from Vertical Limit?"

"No."

"I assume you were going to do a couple more jobs for them. I was supposed to be a guide through the remote parts of Grand Teton and Yellowstone." Though it was uncertain exactly what Mr. Smith's connection to Vertical Limit was, the business checked as being legit in that they sold stock photos. That meant some of the employees might be innocent.

"That's what my contract with them said. I imagine after what happened at the falls, they might shut down or delay."

"Let me see if their website says anything." He scrolled through his phone. The CIA had used the website to track where Vertical Limit sent crews to photograph. It also had a section on upcoming shoots.

Willow rose and stood beside him looking over his shoulder.

The announcement was on the home page.

On May 7, a helicopter accident took the life of a pilot and production coordinator at Glacier Falls, Montana. Our condolences go out to the family members. Future shoots will be delayed until further notice.

Willow took a step back shaking her head. "Vertical Limit says what happened up there was an accident. Why are they lying?"

Quentin's phone rang. Joseph calling him back. "Let me take this." He moved to step back out on the porch. "I may be able to explain everything to you." Hopefully he would have the okay to explain things to Willow.

TEN

As she listened once again to Quentin talking in hushed tones on the porch, Willow felt like she'd been punched in the stomach. She sat down on the couch. Vertical Limit clearly wanted to cover up what had happened at the falls. Her head felt buzzy, like there was a low-level hum in her ears.

Quentin opened the door and stepped back inside. He put his phone in the chest pocket of his shirt.

She locked him in her gaze. "So are you going to explain to me what is going on here?"

He sat down in a chair opposite of her. "Vertical Limit is a front organization. It is a way of moving people around without drawing attention."

"For what purpose?"

"The theft and sale of art, jewelry and artifacts from museums and private collections. The agencies involved in the investigation don't know how many of the Vertical Limit employees are involved or to what degree. We believe the man who was killed, Henry, decided to keep a valuable necklace for himself. It was from a private owner in Italy."

"Why would they lie about what happened up at Glacier Falls? Certainly, there will be a news story. The police saw what happened."

"At best it would be a local news story."

She shook her head still not able to fully comprehend what he was saying. "What are you, like a private investigator?"

"The ring is international. A bunch of agencies are involved. I've been working undercover. I'm with the CIA."

Though she had had her suspicions, the news still stunned her.

"We're so close to catching the man behind the theft ring." He moved from the chair to sit beside Willow on the couch. "The man you saw with the dragonfly tattoo is who we believe is behind the thefts. His code name is Mr. Smith. We are pretty sure he uses Vertical Limit employees as his couriers. If we can catch Mr. Smith, we can end this. And now you have seen him and can remember his face."

"You mean all this time, no one else has seen him?"

"My partner, David Stone, did, right before he was shot by Mr. Smith. He lived long enough to tell me about the tattoo."

"David was important to you?"

"He was a friend and a mentor. You don't work undercover like that and not become close. Mr. Smith was the one who shot him. It would bring closure for me to see him behind bars."

"And I can help you with that because I saw Mr. Smith. Even if he doesn't know how good my memory for faces is, he knows I saw him."

He nodded. "Do you see now why you are in so much danger?"

She nodded, still feeling very numb.

"To the best of our knowledge, you are the only one who has seen Mr. Smith probably without a disguise. We need you to sit down with a forensic sketch artist and then answer some questions. I was just on the phone with my boss setting things up. He gave me permission to tell you this. There is an FBI field office in Helena whose space we can use. They've been briefed on the case."

Willow felt like the walls were closing in on her. The claustrophobia returned. "Guess I don't have much choice."

"I'll drive you there, if you're okay with that. I know you are not crazy about being around me."

"I'm adjusting." Regardless of their romantic history, she knew she was safe with Quentin.

Quentin smiled in response. "Well, that is something."

Her gaze landed on the piece of paper where she'd written down the numbers of the prospective clients for photo jobs. "The sooner I can get back to normal, the better."

His expression changed and he stared at the floor.

It felt as though a heavy weight had been placed on her chest. "I won't be getting back to normal anytime soon, will I?"

"You're probably going to have to stay at a safe house until we can catch Mr. Smith. Maybe until the trial is over."

She burst to her feet and turned away from him. "I don't know if I want to do that."

He stood up as well. His hand gripped her upper

arm, and he turned her around so he could look her in the eyes. "You may have no choice."

"I can't stand the idea of confinement like that. Let me leave the country. I get job offers in South America and Finland. I can stay on the move until the trial…if you catch him."

"He'll find you, Willow. This man is dangerous." He rested his hands on her shoulders. "I know this is way more than you bargained for."

The warmth of his touch seeped through the fabric of her shirt. "There has to be another way besides being cooped up in a house for months."

"Let's take this one step at a time. Come on, I'll drive you to Helena."

She knew Quentin was avoiding the issue she'd raised through diversion. Mr. Smith had been responsible for at least two deaths, one of them her friend Claude. She wanted to see this Mr. Smith caught and brought to justice too. "Can we stop on the way and get my camera gear?"

"Sure. I'd like to talk to the sheriff anyway and find out if they got any prints off of anything."

A picture flashed in her mind. Mr. Smith rummaging through the contents of a backpack while she watched him through the trees. "Mr. Smith was wearing gloves. The thin kind surgeons use so they can still feel things."

Quentin turned toward the door. "Why am I not surprised? He's very good at not getting caught." He glanced back at his father's old landline.

She stood beside him, following the line of his gaze. "Are you still wondering about your dad?"

"He's an adult. He does his own thing. There's a hundred places he could be. I didn't tell him exactly when

I would be by. I might call him later to see if he made it back from wherever."

He stepped out on the porch. She stood in the doorway.

The window beside the door shattered only feet from where she stood. Quentin swung around and piled on top of her, taking her to the floor of the porch. She hit the hard surface with an intense shudder.

"Rifle shot. Get back inside." He rolled off her.

Her heart pounded as her stomach pressed against the hard surface of the porch. She stared through the railing. The shot must have come from the foothills.

She dragged herself on her stomach toward the door and reached up to twist the doorknob. Another shot reverberated through the air. She craned her neck to get a view of Quentin, who lay motionless on his stomach. She wondered if he'd been hit. She gasped.

He turned his head to look at her. "Get inside."

Staying low, she did as she was told. She crawled on all fours, then placed her back against the wall. Quentin pulled himself in, wounded soldier style, a moment later. He positioned himself beside her and pulled his gun out.

Willow gasped for air. "Do you think it's the man we saw in town in the silver car?"

"Probably." Quentin was out of breath as well from all the excitement. "I'm sure he got the information from Mr. Smith that I was from around here. Who knows. He may have asked a couple of locals about me and found out Dad still lived here. I just wonder where he got the rifle."

"He could have brought it with him. He got to Little Horse pretty fast. Do you think he's from around here?"

"Hard to say. Maybe he came here with Mr. Smith and the other guy," said Quentin.

No further shots were fired which made Willow wonder if the shooter was moving in closer to have a better chance of picking them off.

"What if we made a run for the car? We should probably do it before he has a chance to get closer or shoot the tires out, don't you think?"

Quentin ran his hands through his hair, something he did when he was agitated. "He's expecting us to come out the front door, and he's probably lining up the next shot for that. Let's go out the back door and come out on the far side of the car. That way we can use the car as a barrier between us and the rifleman."

He raised his head up so he could peer just above the windowsill.

"Can you see him?"

Quentin stared a moment longer. "I don't see him, but the horses are acting pretty stirred up. My guess is he's by the corral."

Her heart pounded against her ribs. "That's really close."

He sat back down. "We better hurry." He crawled across the living room floor.

Willow followed behind him.

A noise at the other end of the house caused them both to freeze.

"He may be coming through the back door." Quentin's whisper was frantic. "Take cover." She watched Quentin draw his pistol and disappear down the hallway toward where the noise had come from.

Willow glanced around and scrambled toward the kitchen where she grabbed a knife from the butcher block then pressed her back against a lower kitchen cupboard. She braced for the sound of gunfire and prayed for Quentin's safety.

Holding the firearm close to his body, Quentin eased down the hallway with his back to the wall.

The back door swung open toward the outside. At the last second Quentin slipped into a bedroom. He heard footsteps plodding methodically up the hallway toward him. He positioned himself so he would have a view of the man from the back as he passed by the door.

Quentin could hear his own heartbeat drumming in his ears as the footsteps drew closer. Then he saw the man from the back, bald spot, gray hair.

"Dad?"

The older man spun around, eyes wide when he saw the gun. "That's a nice how do you do, son. When did you get into town?"

Quentin put his gun away. There were bruises on Larry Decker's face. "Dad, what happened?"

"You're gone for five years with only the briefest of phone calls to let me know you're alive, and that is how you greet me? I could use a hug, son."

Quentin embraced his dad. "What happened? Where were you?"

"Some yahoo jumped me when I got out of my truck just on the other side of the barn and stole my rifle and took my keys. Knocked me out and tied me up." Larry stepped back and massaged his wrists where the ropes must have been. "'Course I got away. I heard shots being fired. I came back here to call the police."

Their conversation was shattered by the cacophony of glass breaking in the living room.

"Get down. There is a man outside shooting at us with your rifle."

Both men dropped the floor.

Larry shook his head. "I got to hand it to you, son. You do know how to make an entrance after being gone so long."

"Willow is here with me. We need to get her and escape out the back," Quentin said. "You don't move and stay low." There were no windows in the hallway so his dad would be safe. "I'll come back for you."

"Son, you got a lot of explaining to do, but later." He patted Quentin on the back.

Quentin called from the hallway into the living room, using the back of the couch as cover. "Willow, where are you?"

She poked her head around a lower cupboard. "He's getting closer."

Another shot whizzed through the window, breaking more glass. Quentin lifted his head just above the top of the couch. Through the broken window he could see a man running with a rifle and then dropping to the ground behind some hay bales. "I found my dad. Come on, we'll go out the back door and circle around."

Willow crawled on the floor until she met up with him behind the couch. They both made their way down the hallway where they could stand. His father wasn't there anymore. Panic set in. "Dad?"

The old man emerged from a bedroom holding a vintage revolver. "It's not my first rodeo, son. Looked like we could use some fire power." He handed Quentin the holster that would fit his gun.

Quentin took it and shook his head. "Let's go. We

don't have much time. His next move will put him at the edge of the porch."

They hurried down the hallway and out the back door. As they made their way along the side of the house that was the farthest from where the rifleman was, they pressed their backs against the siding.

From what he could remember, he had parked the car pretty close to the porch. That meant there would be only a small window where they would be visible to the shooter. They came to the edge of the house. Quentin peered around the corner but could not see the shooter anywhere. He might still be back by the hay bales or he might have moved in closer.

Quentin gestured to his father and then whispered, "You go first. Get in the back seat. Stay low and scoot over so there is room for Willow. She'll need to get in on the same side so we can use the car for cover."

Larry nodded and bolted the short distance to the car. No shots were fired. Before Larry had even opened the back car door, Quentin gestured for Willow to follow. When she reached the edge of the house, Willow dropped to the ground. From a crouching position, she scrambled the short distance to the cover the car provided. Quentin was right behind her. Making sure to stay below the window line so he wouldn't be seen, he'd gotten into the front seat and started the car just as Willow closed the back door. He had to raise his head slightly to be able to see above the windshield.

A shot went clean through the passenger's side window and out the driver's side window, leaving a hole with a spiderweb pattern around it. If Quentin's head had been two inches higher, it would have taken the bullet. He scrunched down in his seat and backed the car up enough so he could do a forward-facing turn without crashing into the porch. His biggest fear was that the rifleman would shoot out his tires.

He hit the accelerator and caught a flash of movement in his peripheral vision. The shooter was on the move. A gun shot reverberated from inside the car. Larry had scooted to the other side of the back seat, rolled down the window and fired off a round.

"Dad!"

"Told you it wasn't my first rodeo. Just trying to keep him from lining up a shot. Better punch it, son."

Quentin pressed the gas pedal to the floor. He could see the shooter running toward the foothills. He must have parked behind a cluster of trees or maybe even on the other side of the hill to hide his car from view. In any case, it looked like he was going to try to follow them.

Quentin glanced in the back seat. The senior Decker sat back, resting his head on the seat. "Hope I get my rifle back."

As Quentin drew his attention back to the road, Willow laughed. Perhaps it was a tension release over the potential for death they had just managed to escape.

She spoke to Larry, amusement coloring her words. "Glad you're along for the ride."

"Me too."

"Looks like you got a nasty bruise on your cheek."

"Got into a bit of a tussle with the guy who stole my rifle. He knocked me out cold."

"Oh dear. Do you want to go to the ER and make sure there is no permanent damage?"

"Nah, I'll be all right. Thanks for your concern, Willow," Larry said.

His father had always been a tough old rooster.

Rarely visiting the doctor. Despite the circumstances, it was good to be home. He'd missed his father and this part of the world a great deal.

"My son certainly knows how to make an entrance after being gone for five years. What is this all about?"

Quentin tensed as he left the gravel country road and turned onto a two lane. He didn't want his aging father to be in any danger. The less he knew the better. "It's connected to an investigation. That's all I can tell you. Dad, is there a place I can drop you off where you can stay for a few days?"

His father didn't respond right away. "I suppose I can stay with my brother over in Klondike. I won't ask questions. Just glad to see you and Willow are together."

Willow talked in a low voice. "It's not what it looks like, Mr. Decker. Quentin and I are not getting back together as a couple."

"Oh," said Larry. "Sad. Always thought you two were so right for each other. Prayed about it every day for the last five years."

The older man's words echoed through Quentin's mind as he drew his attention to the rearview mirror where several cars were behind him but not close. The only vehicle he could see clearly was a black truck large enough to block the view of the cars behind it. Quentin saw the other cars only for a moment when they were in a curve. The car behind the truck was either white or silver. Hard to tell seeing it for only a second and the sunlight making it difficult to discern the color.

He had to assume they were being followed, and it was just a matter of time before the man in the silver car caught up with them.

ELEVEN

Willow glanced out the back window, expecting to see the silver car zooming toward them. So far, the black truck had stayed a safe distance behind them. Larry sat with his gun in his lap, the barrel pointed toward the car door.

Quentin hit his turn signal when the sign for Klondike where Larry's brother lived came up. The black truck did not follow them. They stopped at the bottom of the exit ramp at the stop sign. No cars followed them.

Klondike had maybe a few hundred people living in town. The farms surrounding it probably consisted of another hundred or so people. Quentin made the turn but had to stop while a train rumbled by.

"When will I be able to go back to the ranch? I got calves I got to keep an eye on."

"Can you get a neighbor to go check on them?"

"For a day or so. You know how it is with a cattle herd, especially right after the babies come along," Larry said.

Quentin chuckled. "Yeah, I remember. I miss that lifestyle. Wouldn't mind getting back to it."

"Could always use the help. I'm not a spring chicken anymore."

Willow's ears perked up. This was the first time Quentin had mentioned wanting to stay in Little Horse. She had assumed his intention was to wrap up his investigation, catch Mr. Smith and go to the end of the earth again for another case.

"I need to give the sheriff back in our county a call. Maybe they can just arrest that guy for assaulting me and stealing my rifle," Larry said.

"You can do that, Dad, but it is more complicated than that."

"I'm sure someday you will explain the whole thing to me."

"Probably not."

The banter between the two men was familiar. The train went by and the fence guard lifted. Quentin rumbled across the tracks. The school came into view. They drove past a post office, a boarded-up store and a thrift shop before turning on a side street. Willow had met Larry's brother only a couple of times. He was quite a few years older and not in good health. When they pulled up to the house with the falling-down fence and the overgrown grass, Willow noticed the curtains move in the living room, but the door did not open.

Larry pushed open his door. "He's going to be crabby that I didn't phone ahead."

"Dad, he's crabby no matter what."

The joke made the elder Decker guffaw. "Call me as soon as I can go back to the ranch, and you and I need to have a sit-down."

"Honestly, Dad, it shouldn't be more than a day."

He poked his head back in the car. "So good to see you, Willow."

"Thanks, Mr. Decker."

Willow got out as well and moved to get in the front seat while Larry made his way through the yard cluttered with car parts and overgrown flower beds.

She closed the passenger's side door.

Quentin waited until his father was safe inside before surging forward and getting turned around.

"It was good to talk with your dad. I've only really seen him to wave or say a quick hello. I'd forgotten what a great sense of humor he has."

Quentin drove back toward the highway. He shook his head. "He's a sharp-witted old guy."

"Did you mean it when you said you were thinking about moving back here and helping with the ranch?"

"I had thought about it. Getting Mr. Smith is personal for me. He killed my partner, my friend. I got into undercover work for the escape and excitement. I'm in a different place now, and I don't want to do this dangerous undercover work anymore."

"But you don't know if you would move back to Little Horse?" The thought of him returning here filled her with anxiety. Maybe it was that she too had run away, only it looked a little different. Almost from the day Quentin had left town, she had sought out one exciting assignment after another. She couldn't bear to be idle for more than a few days even when her bank account was fat.

"I just know I'm ready to not put my life on the line every day." He sped up as they got out on the highway.

They drove past a rest stop. Seconds later, she noticed that silver car behind them. "Looks like he found us."

Quentin accelerated as the silver car drew closer to

them. "Of course, he waited knowing there was only one way out of town."

Several cars going in the other direction whizzed past them.

A sign came up saying the next town was ten miles away. They were about forty minutes from Helena. "Can't we just call the local cops and tell them this guy is harassing us and took shots at us?"

The needle on Quentin's speedometer topped out at eighty. "We can't prove he shot at us. All they could do is question him. They wouldn't be able to hold him. I have the feeling he would run before they could catch up with him anyway."

"What if he still has your dad's rifle? We could get the police to charge him with theft."

"Maybe that would work if he still has the rifle. Putting this guy in jail for a day won't help. Mr. Smith will just send someone else." Quentin adjusted his hands on the steering wheel. "You have to understand. He won't give up until we're both dead."

Willow didn't answer. What could she say? His words sent a chill through her. The silver car drew closer. Quentin hit the blinker when the exit sign for the town of Crystal Springs came up.

"Maybe we can shake him. My gas tank is almost empty anyway."

"What if he's just waiting for us to get back on the highway like he did before?"

"We need to see if there is a back road we can take to get to Helena." Crystal Springs consisted of a convenience store that had two gas pumps. Some houses and trailers were behind the store. There was only one other car parked by the convenience store. He handed

Willow his phone. "Can you bring up a map of the area and see what our options are?"

She took the phone from him and clicked through until she found a map that showed the roads leading into Helena. It was possible there was a road that wouldn't even come up on the map. There were plenty of roads around there that farmers and other locals knew about, little dirt two lanes that would intersect with major roads at some point.

Quentin got out and filled his gas tank. Though the gun he had in his holster was concealed under his jacket, she noticed that he touched it almost as an involuntary movement. He was still on high alert. She scrolled through the map trying to zero in on Crystal Springs.

He tapped on her window. She startled, placing her palm on her chest. She took a moment to recover before rolling down her window.

"Sorry, didn't mean to make you jump. Do you want something to eat and drink?"

"Just a water and anything with protein would be great."

"Lock the doors."

She cranked the handle so her window was shut. Then she reached over to the driver's side to press the button to lock all the doors at once.

She glanced out at the street that ran past the store. A kid on a bike rolled by staring at her. She glanced up the street and behind her. No other cars were on the road. She studied the map on the phone, her vision blurred. Feeling like they were under siege, that at any moment they might be shot at or running for their life was getting to her. She rested her head against the back of the seat.

Tears warmed the corners of her eyes. She swiped at them and turned her attention back to the map on the phone but couldn't bring the image into focus.

Quentin leaned over so his face was visible in the driver's side window. She reached over and unlocked the doors. He stared at her through the glass and then walked around the front of the car to where she was.

He opened the door. "You're not okay, are you?"

He always had been good at reading her emotional state even when she was trying to hide it. She broke down and started to cry. He patted her back. She stood up and he gathered her into his arms and held her while the tears flowed.

Her cheek brushed against the soft fabric of his cotton shirt. And he rested his hand on her head.

"I talked to the guy in the store. There's an old country road we can take that will bring us ten miles outside Helena. We'll get your statement and description and then get you to a safe house."

She pulled away from his embrace and tilted her head to look into his eyes. "I really don't want to go to a safe house."

"We need to take Mr. Smith into custody. Once the trial is over, you won't need protection."

"And if you don't catch him. What will you do? Put me in witness protection? I can't live that way. I don't want to lose the life I have here."

He wiped away a tear from her cheek. The tenderness of the gesture made her feel like she was melting. To be held and comforted by him felt so right.

"Let's cross that bridge when we get to it."

She knew he was avoiding dealing with the issue that concerned her the most, but she decided just to let it go. She handed him his phone back. "Leave it to a local to know where the back roads were. Way more reliable than phone maps."

He took the phone and walked around the hood of the car, grabbing the bag of food he must have put there when he'd come to her side of the car. Once inside, he offered her the bag of groceries.

"There's an iced coffee in there. Can you open it for me and put it in the holder?"

She obliged and then opened the flavored water he'd gotten her along with a peanut butter protein bar.

He rolled through the tiny town past houses that looked to be in need of repair and a community center where children played outside. Rain started to fall as he peered through the windshield. "The road should be around here somewhere."

He took a sip of his coffee while she gulped the water which tasted so good. The moment caused a feeling of nostalgia for her.

How many road trips had they taken together from the time they'd met? Trips to church camps when they were in high school and hikes and kayaking trips. Of course, Luke had been on most of those trips with them.

There was no going back to yesterday. In many ways, Quentin seemed a more mature man than the one who had run away five years ago. She'd spent so much time being angry at him. Maybe her inability to deal with her grief had driven him away. She bore responsibility too.

They could not undo the damage of the past. She wondered if they could move forward and find some way to heal.

Staring out at the rain hitting the window relaxed

her. She closed her eyes and rested her cheek against the back of the seat.

The car slowed even more and then stopped altogether.

The windshield wipers continued to beat out a soothing rhythm.

"Looks like we're not going this way," said Quentin.

Willow opened her eyes and sat up to see what had stopped Quentin.

TWELVE

Quentin stared out at the giant mud hole where the country road had been washed out. "That looks really deep and slick. I can't risk getting stuck."

"There has been a lot of rain this spring. I'm sure the road only gets worse. These roads are not a priority for maintenance." Willow's hand fluttered to her neck as fear entered her voice. "Guess that means we have to go on the highway."

He reached over and patted her leg hoping to sound reassuring. "It'll be okay." After getting turned around, the car rumbled back through the small town. Holding her, being able to comfort her, had felt so familiar, like coming home to a warm house with a fire burning.

Up to this point, his focus had been on keeping Willow safe and getting her to a place where she could be questioned and get an artist's rendering of Mr. Smith. It seemed like that would move the investigation forward. He had been playing defense thinking that all they needed to do was avoid the man in the silver car. If they could catch him, he could be questioned too. But that meant putting Willow in danger.

Quentin approached the exit to get back on the highway. Already he could see that Willow was nervous. She wiggled in her seat and pressed her lips together.

He had a flashback of the first time he'd noticed her in the high school cafeteria. The same pensive and worried expression. Though he'd found out later who she was, he'd been drawn to her even then. He and Luke had been on the football team. Once he and Willow started dating, everything about being with her came so naturally. Not like he had to try to be someone he wasn't. Was it possible that two people were meant for each other? He had tried dating a woman he'd met at church once he left Little Horse thinking that it was time to move on. Though the woman was nice, being with her felt stilted and forced.

The rain intensified as he pulled out on the highway.

"I guess it is too much to hope that he wouldn't come after us. He's probably waiting for us at the next rest stop or turnout," Willow said.

"Probably." He knew he couldn't do what he wanted to without Willow's permission. "There might be a way for us to catch him. If we could take him in for questioning, he might give up something about Mr. Smith that would be helpful."

Willow straightened her seat. "You mean like set a trap?"

"It puts both of us at risk, but it means at least Mr. Teeth won't be on our tail."

"You said Mr. Smith will just send someone else."

"It will take him a while to regroup. We don't know where he and his henchman in the yellow shirt are hiding out. I suspect somewhere close until the mission is completed."

Willow glanced out the side window. She must be mulling over what he was saying.

He glanced in the rearview mirror. "Like you said, if he still has the rifle, we can get highway patrol to come pick him up."

Behind him the silver car was barely discernable in the rain. Its headlights gave off a murky golden glow.

She craned her neck to look out the back window. Her voice was a hoarse whisper. "He found us."

"I can tell you that the intel on Mr. Smith suggests he is running out of people to do his dirty work for him since we pinpointed Vertical Limit as being linked to the thefts. He's getting nervous and desperate which means he might make a mistake."

She still didn't say anything. She laced her fingers together and rested them on her stomach. "Should we call the police and let them know what is happening?"

"Yes, just tell them we think we see the man who stole a rifle and give the description of the car. They will probably dispatch a highway patrolman."

Willow made the call referencing the mile marker they had just passed.

Aware that that they could hydroplane with the deluge of rain coming down, Quentin sped up. He dared not press the pedal to the floor even though the silver car closed the distance between.

"The only way this ends for me is if Mr. Smith is brought into custody, right? Let's not just rely on highway patrol. What is your plan?"

The silver car swerved and slowed down, probably realizing how dangerous speed was in such conditions.

Quentin said, "This road gets curvy in a few miles, if I remember correctly."

Clearly nervous, she wiggled in her seat. "Yes, I think so."

"We need to get far enough ahead to stage what looks like a crash without him seeing it. He'll come after us. One of us will wait in the car with the hazards going and the other will hide not far away waiting to ambush him."

"Let me guess. I'm the one who is in the car and you're the one in the bushes with the gun?"

"That is what would work best." Even though the road had become curvier, Quentin maintained his speed. "We might not be able to make this happen if he tails us too closely. Then we have to hope he doesn't evade highway patrol."

He concentrated on his driving as the speedometer edged past seventy. Willow's silence told him she was afraid, but the lack of protest meant she was on board with the plan. She had always been someone who spoke her mind without reservation. It was one of the things he had liked about her.

He pressed the gas as the road straightened a bit. The silver car was nowhere in sight. Now was their chance. Up ahead, he saw a cluster of trees. "I'll do a soft crash. He'll see you in the passenger seat and assume I'm slumped down in the driver's seat. If it looks like he will stop his car and aim from a distance with the rifle, bail out of the driver's side and come to me."

She nodded. "I'll hit the hazards, so you have time to hide. From a distance, I can make it look like I am unconscious."

He appreciated how quickly Willow could overcome her fear and get on board with the plan. Risking the life of a civilian was outside his training's playbook. If it had been anyone else besides Willow, he wouldn't have done it. Years spent with her in high-risk situations like back country skiing and rock climbing told him she was cool under fire.

He accelerated into a gradual turn and ripped the wheel sideways as he pumped the brakes and crossed the center line, aiming the front of the car toward the ditch and the cluster of brush and trees. Though he had lost substantial speed by the time the hood bumped the side of the ditch, the jarring impact to his body still caused a degree of shock and knocked the wind out of him. The impact of the soft crash had not been enough to cause the airbags to deploy.

Willow patted his thigh. "Go, Quentin." She glanced nervously up the road where they had just been.

Grateful that she had recovered from the impact faster than he had, he unclicked his seat belt and pushed the door open. Even before he made it to the trees, he saw the silver car come around the curve and slow down. Quentin dropped down low so his car would keep him concealed.

Willow prayed that Quentin made it to his hiding place in time. The rain had let up some, but she suspected the downpour had made everything a little muddy. She also prayed that the man in the silver car wouldn't just shoot her through the window at a distance.

What they needed was for him to approach the car and check on the scene. That would buy them precious seconds. Of course, once he saw that Quentin wasn't in the driver's seat, that is when she would need to act. If he was close enough, she could push the door open and hit him with it. She pressed the hazard button and unclicked her seat belt but left it draped across her chest, so it looked like she was still secured. She rolled down the window a couple of inches so she could hear what was going on. She closed her eyes but intended to take quick glances to gauge what the man was going to do.

Willow caught a flash of the silver car slowing and pulling off on the narrow shoulder only feet from where they were.

Turning her face toward where the other car had stopped, she rested her head against the seat. She closed her eyes but not before registering that the man with the metal teeth had opened his car door. He held a gun at his side with one hand.

Hopefully, highway patrol had been alerted and was somewhere close.

She heard the car door slam and the scrunch of footsteps on gravel as he approached. Her heart pounded in her chest as she tried not to move, to appear unconscious and vulnerable.

The footsteps stopped. Her heartbeat pulsed in her ears. Her eyes shot open. Metal Teeth had not yet lifted the gun to aim.

Quentin shouted, "Drop the weapon and put your hands in the air where I can see them."

Her eyes shot open. Metal Teeth smiled as he aimed the gun at her. "Do you really think you can get a shot off before I take her out?"

Quentin's response was to fire his weapon, hitting the man's hand that held the gun. The man doubled over, gripping his hand and dropping the pistol. With his gun still drawn, Quentin stood on the driver's side of the car by the corner of the hood. To try to move around the front of the car would be awkward. The slant of the ditch could distract him from keeping the red dot of his laser beam sight on Metal Teeth.

Willow pushed open the door, preparing to move forward and grab the dropped gun before Metal Teeth could recover and reach for it. Even as she scrambled the short distance across the gravel shoulder, she watched his uninjured hand which was within inches of the gun. Was he foolish enough to think Quentin wouldn't shoot him?

Everything seemed to move in slow motion as Willow realized the laser dot was bouncing around. She glanced over her shoulder. In an effort to get around the hood of the car and get closer to the shooter, Quentin had stumbled. The ground might be slick from the rain. She dove toward the other man, body slamming him so he fell on the ground. He hit the hard earth with a thud and a grunt.

When she looked up, Quentin had recovered and was stalking toward them, gun drawn.

"Good work, Willow."

She rolled away from Metal Teeth and reached for the gun where it still lay.

Quentin addressed the man on the ground. "Put your hands up where I can see them and rise slowly." He kept his eyes on Metal Teeth but tilted his head toward Willow. "There should be some zip ties in the trunk. Can you get some?"

Metal Teeth held his hands up and flashed a grin. "Zip ties. How handy. You also seem very proficient with a gun. Almost like you're a cop or something."

Willow caught the tone of suspicion in the man's voice. It did make Quentin look like law enforcement to have those on hand. Though zip ties were used for other things.

"Force of habit. I used to be a deputy in this county."

Willow could still hear the conversation as she opened the driver's side door to push the trunk button.

"You never know when you're going to have to make a citizen's arrest, right?" From his tone, it was clear Metal Teeth still had not let go of his suspicions.

Willow opened the trunk and spotted the zip ties right away. She had no idea what was going to happen with Quentin and his investigation. Would he go back undercover? It wasn't just the zip ties but the way Quentin conducted himself that screamed he was law enforcement. Would Metal Teeth buy that it was just because Quentin used to be a deputy?

She walked toward Quentin, who kept the gun trained on Metal Teeth.

"What about my car?"

"We'll arrange to have it towed. Now turn around and put your hands behind your back." Once the man complied, he addressed his comments to Willow in a much softer voice. "Can you secure his hands, please?"

Willow stepped toward the man when his hands were in place. She put the zip tie cuffs on him and made sure they were secure but not too tight.

While the man's back was turned, Quentin gave Willow a raised eyebrow and then glanced up the road, probably wondering if highway patrol would show up. "Can you check his car for my father's rifle? I suppose we will let the police handle this. My guess is he will be charged with theft at the very least."

"Why don't you handle it?" said Metal Teeth. "You act like you know a thing or two about being a cop."

Like I said, I used to be." Quentin must have picked up on the man's insinuations and now was trying to cover his tracks.

"I think you might be a little more than some hapless local guy," said Metal Teeth.

As she walked over to the silver car, she realized that the man could be out of jail very quickly if all they could charge him with was theft. What if he communicated with Mr. Smith about his suspicions concerning Quentin?

They placed Metal Teeth in the back seat and the rifle in the trunk.

The rain had become no more than a drizzle as she watched Quentin pace and talk on the phone trying to find out if highway patrol was anywhere close.

Not wanting to get any wetter she got into the front seat of the car.

From the back, Metal Teeth grunted. "Do you think I don't know what is going on here?"

The menace in his voice made her breath catch in fear. "I don't know what you're talking about."

She heard the creak of the vinyl seat and then Metal Teeth's voice was even louder and closer to her. A move designed to intimidate her.

"That guy may be an ex-cop, but I say he's working on something. Once a cop, always a cop."

Though she struggled to keep the terror out of her voice and sound calm, Willow decided to play the innocent. "You know, it's been five years since I've seen him. I have no idea what he is up to. All he told me was he came back here for a job as a guide for Vertical Limit."

Quentin had clicked off the phone and was making his way back to car.

"Sure, sure." Came the threatening voice from the back seat.

Quentin got into the car. The glance he gave Willow didn't communicate anything clearly to her.

Quentin stared into the rearview mirror. "What is your name, sir?"

"Scott. You don't need to know my last name."

"Well, Scott, I just talked to the police. I will be dropping you off at their office. You will be charged with theft of my father's rifle and transported to the county where the theft took place."

"How very official of you. I'll be out on bail before the day is over."

Quentin didn't say anything, though she could see the vein pulsing in his temple. He was nervous too. He started the car and pulled out onto the road.

She only hoped that Quentin had found a way to keep Scott from going free. If Mr. Smith knew Quentin was working undercover, that would make it even harder to catch him. He might even go into hiding and never be caught.

THIRTEEN

Quentin drove to the city police building. When he opened up the back door, Scott grinned at him. Features as distinctive as metal teeth would make it easy to see if Scott was connected to any of the other international thefts, either with the transport or the sale of the stolen items. It could be that Scott knew very little and was just a hired gun who happened to be close by when Mr. Smith needed help. The important thing was that Scott not be allowed to communicate with Mr. Smith.

His phone call had been to his colleague at the FBI who was waiting inside the city police building to take Scott into custody. From there, Scott would be transported and held in a separate place from where Quentin was taking Willow. Scott would be questioned by another agent to find out what his level of contact with Mr. Smith had been.

"Come on, let's go."

Scott scooted across the seat, and Quentin helped him get out of the car and stand by gripping the back of his shirt and pulling him up. He shielded and tilted Scott's head with his hand so he didn't bang into the roof of the car.

Once he was on his feet, Scott gave Quentin a look filled with anger, but he did not resist as Quentin led him into the police station and handed him off to the officer who was waiting inside. He'd find out later if Scott had given up anything that might be useful to the investigation.

Quentin returned to the car where Willow was waiting. With Scott gone, they could talk freely. He checked the address for the FBI field office on his phone and typed it into his GPS.

He started the car but did not shift into Drive. "You doing okay?"

She played with the zipper of her jacket. "So what happens now?"

"I'll drop you off. One of the agents will question you about anything you can remember concerning Mr. Smith, and they will call in a sketch artist to help you put together a picture of him."

"Where are you going to be?"

"I have to make a phone call to assess how and if we move this investigation forward with me undercover," Quentin said.

Still clutching the zipper of her jacket, she stared out the window. "But you'll be in the building?"

He shifted into Drive and pressed the gas, wondering what was going on inside her head. Things had changed for the better. A day ago, she acted like she couldn't get away from him fast enough. "I'm not sure what is going to happen to be honest with you, Willow."

"But for sure, they're going to put me in a safe house?"

So that was what she was primarily concerned about.

The GPS warned him to get ready for a turn in a hundred feet. The click click of his blinker seemed unusually loud. "We don't have a lot of choice here. We need you safe."

"I would rather be in danger than be confined like some kind of prisoner. The one thing that has helped me deal with what happened five years ago was the ability to be on the move, to always be looking forward to a new location and a new shoot."

He made the turn. No matter what, they were always circling back to five years ago. The GPS informed him that his location was on the right. He turned into the parking lot of the brick office building that seemed to house other offices besides the FBI field office.

He stopped the car, pulled the key out and undid his seat belt so he could look Willow in the eyes. "If there was any other way, I would do it."

She turned slightly and let out a heavy breath. "I need to go back to work. I have bills to pay."

The protest was a last-ditch effort not to face the confinement of a safe house. "The agency has funds for people in safe houses. I'm not sure how all that works."

She shifted in her seat.

He leaned over and squeezed her shoulder. "I'll stay with you until we can get everything set up if that helps. I imagine the sketch artist needs to be called in since I could not give them an exact time when we would arrive."

Though she seemed to be softening toward him, he wasn't sure if she would take him up on his offer given her animosity when they had first been reunited.

"I'd like that, Quentin." She pressed the tab of her seat belt and pulled it off her body. The smile she gave him was warm and genuine.

When they entered the building, a man with buzz-cut gray hair and a slender physique stood in a doorway.

"Are you Agent Decker?" He reached his hand out toward Quentin. "I'm Special Agent Linman."

Quentin nodded and touched Willow's shoulder. "This is Willow Farris."

"I've got an interview room all set up. Give me just a minute to let the sketch artist know she's on deck. She has about a ten-minute drive to get here."

Agent Linman retreated to another room, closing the door halfway. They could hear his hushed conversation.

The room they were in contained a desk with a phone and computer and two file cabinets.

"Can I take a minute to check my messages again? I'm concerned Mom might have called. We haven't talked in a while if she has called, and I'm sure she has started to wonder why she hasn't heard from me."

It sounded like Agent Linman had gotten into some chatty conversation with the sketch artist.

"Sure."

Willow sat on the corner of the desk and lifted up the phone and pressed in some numbers. While it dialed through, she spoke to him. "I hope I can get my phone back along with my camera gear soon."

"Sorry that plan got derailed. We can maybe arrange for it to be brought to you."

A mechanical voice on the phone vibrated through the line, and Willow turned her attention back to listening to her messages. The first message sounded like it was a female voice and it made Willow smile and shake her head. Probably her mother. The automated voice spoke again and then another message was played.

Quentin watched Willow's smile fade and all the color drain from her face. The phone line went quiet.

"Willow?"

"That was the rep from Vertical Limit. He wanted to know when I could be back on the job."

Willow felt like the wind had been knocked out of her. She put the phone back in the cradle. Quentin stepped toward her.

Agent Linman poked his head out the door. "Sorry about that. The sketch artist is an old friend." He looked at Willow. "Everything okay?"

Quentin edged closer to Willow and touched her elbow lightly. He looked over at Agent Linman. "Could you give us just a second?"

"Sure, no problem. Whenever you're ready." He slipped back into the interview room.

"Why would they call me and leave a message like that after what happened up at the falls?"

"Not everyone who works for Vertical Limit is on the take. It could be that the rep was told some kind of story and he is just trying to get the shoot back on schedule."

"Or it could be that they are trying to lure me back to set a trap."

Quentin nodded.

She leaned against the desk. "I wonder if they left a message for you as well on your old phone."

"Probably. Did they mention the deaths up at the falls?"

"He just apologized for the delay the *accident* had caused." Willow said. "He might just be an employee who doesn't know what is really going on."

"Are you up to doing this interview and sitting with the sketch artist?"

Her heart wasn't pounding anymore. "I need to sit down. If I could just have a minute to catch my breath. I need to call my mom and let her know I'm okay. I won't tell her anything. I don't want her to worry."

"I'll give you some privacy." Quentin stepped out of the room.

Willow made the call to her mom. Because she was afraid her mother would detect something in her voice if she talked to her, Willow was grateful when the answering machine came on. "Hey, Mom, just wanted to check in. I'm going to be busy for a few days. Love you."

After hanging up, she found Quentin. "I'm ready. Let's do this."

He pointed toward the room where Agent Linman was.

She stepped in front of him. He rested his hand on her upper back as a way of showing support. Something he used to do years ago.

Agent Linman sat at a table with two empty chairs on the other side. "You look as though you've had a shock."

Willow pulled one of the chairs out. "I'll be okay."

Quentin crossed the room to where a watercooler was. He brought Willow a cup of water and set it in front of her.

"I think I will be staying for the interview if you don't mind," Quentin said.

"Sure, no problem. We have a standard set of questions that might help identify the man you saw. We need to try to prod your memory not just for appearance but anything in his mannerism that was distinct." Agent Linman looked toward Quentin who had taken the seat next to Willow. "My understanding is that the information will be sent to CIA headquarters."

Quentin nodded. "We're hoping that he may have

appeared in some of the surveillance photos we have collected over the course of the investigation."

Willow took a sip of her water. The cool liquid was soothing. "I think I'm ready."

Agent Linman opened a laptop sitting on the table. "We'll stop and take a breather anytime you need to. The questions are designed to jog your memory."

She gripped the cup and took another sip of water. Quentin scooted a little closer to her and rested his arm on the back of her chair.

Agent Linman asked the first few questions which were about Mr. Smith's build and general demeanor. The question about scars and tattoos was easy enough to answer.

Quentin leaned forward. "We might get the sketch artist to do a separate image of the tattoo. If it's distinct enough we could maybe trace it back to the artist who did it, anything to give us a line on this guy."

Agent Linman nodded and continued with his questions. The one thing that surprised her as she tried to bring up the picture in her mind of Mr. Smith was that she realized that his blond hair was dark at the roots, probably dyed. She remembered too that he had distinctive green eyes but wondered if they were contact lenses because the color was too intense to be natural.

The sketch artist arrived and waited outside until the interview was done.

Agent Linman wrapped up his questions and closed his laptop. He called in the sketch artist and excused himself.

"I'm Janet Paige. I work with the police department." She sat where Agent Linman had been and pulled out a tablet of paper as well as some pencils and charcoal.

She looked at Quentin and then Willow. "I'm only doing a drawing from your description, correct?"

Willow turned to face Quentin. "You stayed with me for support. But I'm okay if you need to make some phone calls."

Quentin rose from his chair. He gave her shoulder a squeeze on his way out.

Janet arranged her art materials. "I know there are computer programs now that help sketch artists, but I really would rather do it the old-fashioned way. I used to be an officer myself before I retired. Always enjoyed sketching and painting."

Willow guessed that Janet was in her late fifties. She was dressed in a Western-cut shirt and jeans. "The man had a really distinctive dragonfly tattoo. It was suggested that I try to describe that as well."

Janet flipped open her artist's tablet. "Sure, why don't we start with the face."

Willow could see Mr. Smith in her mind as though he were out of focus.

Janet had already begun to sketch. "Eyes are usually a good place to start. Shape? How far apart?"

Janet asked questions and showed Willow what she came up with and made adjustments. The face she'd seen in the forest came to life. Once Janet was finished, she tore the completed drawing from the tablet. "It's my understanding that there is some sort of interagency investigation going. Agent Linman will send this to the powers that be."

Willow shrugged. "All I know is that I was supposed to recall the features of the man I saw at the falls."

They moved on to the dragonfly tattoo.

As Janet's pencil swirled across the paper making

soft scratching sounds, an idea began to form in Willow's mind. What if she did go back to work for Vertical Limit and help Quentin track down Mr. Smith? Though she knew it would take some energy to convince Quentin, it would mean she wouldn't have to be confined in the safe house.

FOURTEEN

After exchanging some small talk with Agent Linman, Quentin was directed to a quiet room down a hallway where he could make his phone call uninterrupted. Rather than talking to his handler, he dialed his supervisor directly. The news that Vertical Limit wanted Willow to come back and work for them was upsetting.

Agency research on Vertical Limit had not located a home office. An audit had uncovered that the company was an LLC that filed taxes in the United States. An examination of employee records revealed an ever-changing staff and no CEO. The person who had filed the papers of incorporation was now deceased. The stock photo company often employed freelancers. If they could attach an identity to Mr. Smith, they might be able to figure out what his connection to Vertical Limit was.

Quentin pressed in the number of his supervisor and waited until Dan Ormoff picked up. Quentin summarized everything that had happened, including taking Scott into custody, the message that Willow had received and the need to get at least a short-term safe house set up for her.

Dan paused before responding. "So chances are that if Willow got a message to come back to work, you did too on the phone you no longer have, correct?"

"Probably, yes."

"You have a contact number?"

"I don't have it memorized, but it's listed on their website. I can get hold of the man who left a message for Willow and see if they want me back."

"You're sure your cover hasn't been blown?"

Quentin paced as he talked. "Reasonably sure they just think I'm a guy from this area who answered an ad for a guide. Scott, the hired gun whom we took into custody, suspects something. We need to make sure he remains in jail and can't communicate with anyone."

"Two of the jewels from that stolen necklace turned up in an unrelated drug raid in Idaho. The guy said he bought it off a fence a week ago. That was the same time Vertical Limit was in Idaho doing a shoot, and Henry was the point man."

That news only confirmed to Quentin that the best way to catch Mr. Smith or learn more about him was to go where Vertical Limit went. "Do you think Henry held on to the necklace and was parting it out?"

"Probably. If another jewel shows up, we know it's in someone else's hands," said Dan.

"Why go to so much trouble to kill Henry if he hadn't decided it was more profitable to work for himself?"

"Or maybe Henry delivered the necklace like he was supposed to, but he was getting cold feet and was about to squeal."

"No, I don't think that is what was going on. From what Willow said, Mr. Smith was clearly looking for something up at the falls. In the brief time I was with him, Henry mentioned being nervous about his finances. There wasn't enough time to build some trust and get a confession out of him," Quentin said.

"All we can do is speculate. I think the most important thing is for you to get back in there and see what you can find out."

"I can do that. The next shoot is scheduled for a remote part of Yellowstone. I used to hike the back country up there all the time. I'm sure they would be hard pressed to find another guide on such short notice."

"I want to go too." A voice sounded behind him.

He swung around. Willow stood in the doorway.

He'd been so focused on his conversation with his back to the door, he hadn't realized she was there.

"Is someone with you?" Dan asked.

Quentin spoke into the phone. "Just a second." He pulled the phone away from his face. "Willow, no."

"They won't be able to find a photographer on such short notice. And then it will be canceled. You'll lose your chance to find out what is really going on."

She had a point.

Quentin spoke into the phone. "Listen, Dan, I'll call you back." He disconnected and then put his phone down. "It's too dangerous, Willow."

"The sooner we track down Mr. Smith, the sooner I can have my life back. I'm not going to spend the rest of my life as a prisoner separated from everyone and everything I love or looking over my shoulder."

"It might not come to that."

"But it could. That's not a chance I want to take. We have to catch Mr. Smith."

"There is too much potential for you to get hurt…or worse. I can't put you in harm's way like that."

"You'd be there with me. That's the best protection I know."

Her words warmed his heart. It meant so much to him that she had gotten back to a place of deep trust with him. "I appreciate that, but I still say no."

"The last time Mr. Smith wanted to do away with Henry, he waited until he was in an isolated spot. Mr. Smith has made it clear that he wants to get rid of me. What if he tries a similar ambush to get to me? We could set a trap."

He felt drawn to her for her courage. She saw the two of them as a team, at least where this investigation was concerned. She was willing to be bait to catch Mr. Smith.

He shook his head. "I could never forgive myself if something happened to you, Willow."

"Look, I signed a contract that said I'd do the Yellowstone shoot. I need to keep my word."

Putting her life in danger to keep her word was hardly a good point. He saw the expression of determination and knew it would be hard to talk her out of what she wanted to do.

"Give me a second to call my boss back. If we can find another way to make this investigation go forward without risking harm to you, that would be my preference."

She nodded and disappeared down the hallway. Quentin paced, picked up his phone and then put it back down. There was a window with the blinds pulled in the office where he was. He peered outside. This part of the building looked out on a small park. There was a large parking lot and beyond that a strip mall. He watched the shoppers' activity for a moment trying to decide what to do.

Willow was right. If she didn't come with him as the

photographer, the shoot might be canceled altogether, and he would lose his opportunity to snoop around while undercover. Whoever they sent from Vertical Limit might be the lead they were looking for. And if they could draw Mr. Smith out and catch him, the investigation would be closed.

He picked up the phone and pressed in Dan's number. Dan answered right away.

Quentin cut to the punch. "Willow Farris wants to go undercover with me as the photographer for this next shoot."

"That sounds risky. Putting a civilian in danger like that."

"I agree, but the thing is Mr. Smith wants her out of the picture. He's made that clear. Given how he hasn't been successful so far, we think he might use the remote location to go after her. I know it's short notice, but if we could get some backup in place following us to the location and then maybe already positioned at the location, we might even be able to catch Mr. Smith before he goes after Willow."

"You think he will show up himself?"

"He did at Glacier Falls."

"It's your call. You are the one who knows Willow," said Dan.

Quentin's stomach knotted. "I don't know what to do. This might be our last window of opportunity."

"Another agent could pick up the trail."

"Maybe...but not likely. I have a feeling Mr. Smith utilizing Vertical Limit as a cover might be coming to an end. When he made an appearance up at the falls, it was an indication that he might be running out of people to recruit to do his dirty work. What if he goes even deeper underground and finds some new way to run his operation? We'll never get him. That means Willow would have to be looking over her shoulder for the rest of her life or go somewhere she can't be found. I know she doesn't want that."

"What is your assessment of Willow Farris?"

"That she can handle herself just fine. That she is cool under fire."

Dan said, "I know you intended to leave the agency once this case is wrapped up. I'm sure you would like it to be sooner rather than later."

"Thanks, Dan. I'll communicate with you as soon as I decide what the plan is." He clicked off the phone and set it on the table. Even though the blinds were still drawn, he looked toward the window where normal life was unfolding outside. Shoppers were going into the strip mall. People were visiting. Children were getting new shoes or a book. He longed to get back to normal life and for Willow to have that too.

Quentin leaned against the table and massaged the space between his eyebrows. All these competing motives and goals. He wasn't sure what to do.

He heard footsteps on the carpet. Even without turning around, he knew Willow was standing in the doorway.

"If it's any consolation, the decision is mine and mine alone. I'm responsible for myself and my safety. If something happens to me, it won't be your fault. I am signing up for this undercover work for my own selfish reasons. I want this guy caught so I don't have to spend years in hiding and afraid."

Quentin turned around to face the woman he had once loved. "You know I can't just let go of that responsibility. It's not in my nature."

* * *

Willow saw such warmth in Quentin's eyes, she stepped toward him into the room. "I get that. Let's do this together so we can both get back to the life we want."

He nodded. "Let me call the rep at Vertical Limit who left the message for you. Just to clarify that he wants me back as well. I'll just tell him the truth, that I lost my phone up by the falls. Talking to him will give me a chance to discern if he knows anything or if he is just a clueless employee who schedules photo shoots." He reached out and rubbed her shoulder. "Sound good?"

"Sure." She didn't move away from his touch or the magnetic pull of his gaze. They had shared something special years ago, but they had been so young, so unable to deal with a true crisis. Maybe both of them had grown since then. Hard to say.

"Look, it's almost dark. I'm sure Agent Linman can set us up in a temporary safe house overnight."

"I still need to get my camera gear."

"I'll arrange to have it delivered to you in a way that would keep Mr. Smith and his cohorts from tracking us there."

"I suppose I can stand one night at a safe house. You'll be there too?" She found herself hoping that they would have enough downtime to talk.

"I'll set things up. Give me just a minute to call Vertical Limit and then arrange for your camera gear to be delivered."

As she retreated to the administrative area, Willow could hear Quentin talking in low tones on the phone. Agent Linman was in the interview room with his laptop open.

He looked up when Willow poked her head in.

"The sketch has been sent to your people."

"Actually, they're just Quentin's people. I really am just a photographer. Quentin requested that I ask you if you could arrange for a safe house for us for the night."

"No problem. I can set that up within the hour. Security detail might take a little more time."

"Quentin is going to be with me. That should be enough."

"I don't know what your threat level is here. Quentin hasn't shared the details with me, and maybe he can't. Let me get the safe house set up for you."

Willow retreated back to the reception area and waited. Quentin emerged from the second room. "The police left me a message. Your camera gear is on the way. I requested they drop it off at this office. No need to have the locals know where we are staying."

She tensed as she asked the next question. "And what about the photo shoot?"

"Vertical Limit wants me on the shoot tomorrow. The production coordinator will meet us at Old Faithful and we'll drive up to the location from there. We're working to get some backup in place."

Willow tilted her head toward the interview room. "He's setting stuff up for a place to stay overnight."

When it grew quiet in the interview room, Quentin stepped in and spoke to Agent Linman. She could pick up only a few words of the conversation. Something about Agent Linman bringing the camera gear.

Quentin came back into the reception area. "I've got an address for us." He held up a key.

"I'll check in with Agent Linman before we go to

sleep to give him the all clear. Other than that, we're on our own. You okay with that?"

The truth was there was no one other than Quentin that she felt safe with.

Within minutes they were in the car and driving across town in the twilight. The house was in a subdivision with large lots and high fences for privacy.

He handed her the key. "If you would go inside and open the garage door so I can hide the car."

She glanced around the yard as she made her way up the walk to open the door. In the dim light, she fumbled to find the keyhole. She turned the key and twisted the doorknob.

The roar of a car going by on the street startled her. Headlights made her wince, and a sports car made its way up the street, turning into the driveway of a large two-story colonial.

She was still very hypervigilant and aware that they were not totally safe no matter what. She stared back at Quentin's silhouette as he waited in the car. After opening the door, she felt around for a light switch and made her way through the living room toward a door she assumed led to the garage. She pressed the button that would open the garage and stood back while Quentin drove his car in. Once the car was inside, she closed the garage.

She waited for him, and they returned to the living room together. The house looked like it had been furnished off the showroom floor and that everything had been a matching set. The pictures on the wall were like something from a doctor's office. Nothing homey or cozy about the place.

"This house is set up as a vacation rental, so the

neighbors aren't alarmed when it's empty or they see new faces." Quentin walked over and opened an entryway closet.

"That's a really smart setup." All the drapes and blinds were pulled shut. Willow clicked on several lights.

"The cupboards should be stocked if you're hungry." Quentin moved to the window, drew back the curtain and peered outside. "We got here on such short notice, I doubt there is anything fresh in the refrigerator."

She opened cupboards which were brimming with canned goods, noodles, spices and spaghetti sauce. There was a loaf of bread in the freezer along with some hamburger. The refrigerator was empty. She'd noticed some of the dried parmesan cheese in the cupboard and olive oil. "I think I could manage poor man's spaghetti with some garlic toast."

When she checked the clock on the microwave, it was almost 8:00 p.m.

Quentin stepped into the kitchen. "I can give you a hand if you like."

She pulled the bread and the beef out of the freezer. "Sure. It will take a second to thaw out the hamburger." She pulled down some of the other ingredients.

Quentin rooted around in a lower cupboard and came up with some soft drinks. "I can put ice in some glasses if you want while the rest of the carton gets cold."

He poured her some grape soda while she started browning the beef. They worked without talking much. Quentin found a can opener and grabbed the can of tomatoes. He also located a pot to boil the spaghetti noodles in.

Once the garlic toast came out of the oven, they sat down to eat at the table Quentin had set. He grabbed each of them another soda. Sitting opposite each other, they bowed their heads while Quentin said a prayer of thanks.

They ate, making small talk about the meal. For not being made from fresh ingredients, it tasted pretty good. Maybe it was because she hadn't eaten anything substantial since Quentin had made her the grilled cheese. She found herself enjoying the flavors.

When both of their plates were nearly empty, and she wasn't jittery from hunger anymore, she put her fork down and laced her hands together. How did she begin to talk with Quentin about the accident that had taken her brother's life? At least now she felt like she was finally ready to talk without being angry or consumed by sorrow.

Outside, she could see through the slits in the blinds the headlights of a car rolling up the street. The car stopped outside their house.

Quentin rose to his feet. "Get to the bedroom and lock the door. Wait for me to give you the all clear."

She assumed the bedroom must be up the stairs. Maybe it had been foolhardy not to look around to become familiar with the layout.

Her breathing intensified as she went partway up the stairs. Quentin pulled his gun out of the holster and headed toward the window by the front door.

FIFTEEN

The car had parked on the street by the safe house. Quentin crouched beneath the windowsill. By peering between the blinds, he had a limited view of the street. The car engine was turned off as were the headlights. No one got out.

His heart pounded while he waited and watched. He could see no one else on the street though he did notice the glow of television sets in two windows. Everyone must have turned in for the night.

His phone, which he'd left on the table, dinged that he had a text message. The sound was one that almost compulsively made a person want to pick up the phone and check the screen. It occurred to him that only four people had his new phone number: Agent Linman, the rep from Vertical Limit, his handler and his supervisor.

"I can check it if you want." The voice was Willow's. She must be on the stairs.

"I told you to go up to the bedroom."

"I thought you might need some backup."

He heard her footfalls on the stairs and then she was looking at him from across the room. He peered out the window again. The car was still sitting across the street.

Though it was too dark to see the driver's face, he could discern that the driver hadn't gotten out of the car.

"Turns out you do need my help. I can check your message for you." She walked across the floor.

"Willow, stay low."

She dropped to the ground and reached up for the phone while crouching by the table. She stared at the phone and then laughed. "It's all clear, Quentin. That is Linman outside. He has my camera gear. He says to open the garage door and he will set the gear inside, so we don't have to go out and make an appearance in case we're being watched or have somehow been tracked to this neighborhood."

Smart. Quentin holstered his gun. Making an appearance outside might draw attention from the neighbors who would be able to describe them if one of Mr. Smith's men showed up later.

"You stay put," Quentin said. "I'll open the garage door."

Willow pulled out a dining room chair and sat down.

Quentin entered the garage and pressed the panel to open the door. He slipped back into the shadows before the door was completely open. He could hear footsteps and things being placed on the ground. Linman had to make two trips.

"You're good," said Linman.

Quentin waited for the other man to back out before shutting the garage door. He flipped on the light and carried the first three bags of gear into the living room. Willow rushed toward him like he was holding her long-lost child.

"I'm so glad to have my stuff back."

He sat the totes on the living room floor, taking the

strap of the last bag off his shoulder. Willow was already sorting through her stuff when he went back to the garage to get the second load which included two tripods.

Willow had laid out several lenses and a camera and was sorting through a smaller tote when he returned and set the remainder of the gear down. "I got to get this reorganized for maximum efficiency. If I remember correctly, we have a bit of a hike to get to the location."

Growing up he and Willow had treated Yellowstone like their backyard.

"A short hike," Quentin said. He watched Willow for a moment. She seemed pretty focused on what she was doing. He was suddenly aware of how fatigued he was. "I'll clear those dishes in a moment. I'm just going to sit down and rest my eyes."

He collapsed in an easy chair and closed his eyes before Willow responded. "Yeah, I'll give you a hand with that as soon as I'm done here."

Quentin drifted off to the sound of Willow packing up her gear.

He awoke in darkness and quiet. Outside, car headlights eased by on the street. He fumbled in the darkness looking for the lamp by the couch. A moment later the car rolled back down the street going in the opposite direction. Someone looking for something at a very odd hour?

He stumbled into the kitchen. The clock on the microwave said it was four in the morning. Willow had cleared the dishes herself. The camera gear was neatly arranged in two separate piles. And her phone was plugged in and charging. Probably one pile was what she intended to take with her to the location and the other was what she would leave in the car.

Chances were, they wouldn't be coming back to this safe house.

When he checked his phone, he had several voice messages from Dan who had pulled together some backup for him. A car with an FBI agent would be waiting and watching in the lot by Old Faithful where they planned to pick up the production coordinator. That car would follow them up at a distance. There would be an agent hiding at the site of the shoot before they got there.

He climbed the stairs, passing a room with a closed door which must be the bedroom Willow had chosen. He found a room at the end of the hall with an attached bathroom. He was glad to see that there was toothpaste and a supply of unopened toothbrushes. He needed a shower but was too tired to deal with that until morning. He brushed his teeth and splashed some water on his face before crawling underneath the soft comforter.

He had no idea what tomorrow held. They needed to be braced for almost anything. As he drifted off to sleep, he found himself hoping that he and Willow would find time to talk about the past. It felt like both of them were ready for that.

He had decided for sure that once this case was wrapped up, he would return to help his aging father with the ranch. She seemed softer toward him now. If they were going to live in the same town maybe they could at least find a way to be friends.

He pulled the blanket around his shoulders and prayed that tomorrow would bring some solutions to the investigation without bloodshed.

* * *

The morning sun sneaked in through the slits in the blinds, but it was the smell of Italian spices that lured Willow out of bed and down the stairs.

Quentin looked a little comical in the frilly apron he must have found somewhere as he stood by the stove. "You hungry? I reheated the spaghetti from last night."

"Starved."

"Wish we could go out for fresh stuff, but why take the chance?"

His comment was a reminder that they were not guests at a bed-and-breakfast but people whose lives were under serious threat.

"I'll set the table."

They sat down to a breakfast of spaghetti and canned peaches. The food was tasty and satisfying. Halfway through the meal, Quentin's phone rang. He looked at the number. "I better take this." He scooted away from the table and wandered into the living room. His back was turned toward her, but she gathered from the snippets of conversation she could hear that he was talking to another agent. She heard the mention of the police sketch and the name Scott Vissor, the man with the metal teeth who had chased them.

Willow finished up her meal, glancing at the camera gear she'd organized. Maybe the day would be uneventful, and she could just enjoy doing what she loved. Her stomach tightened. That was probably too much to hope for.

She gathered up the dishes, leaving Quentin's unfinished plate out. His food would be cold when he came back to it.

Quentin got off the phone. "Good news. Headquarters examined the drawing you gave them. A man with similar facial structure appears in several Vertical Limit photos in European locations. They are trying to track down who he is using facial recognition software." He sat down and picked up his fork. "This is real progress. If we can get a name to go with that face, we should be able to track him down." Quentin finished the rest of his cold meal.

"He changes his appearance. What if he also uses aliases when he travels?"

"The agency will compare passport photos with similar names. We have sorting software that makes that easy. Also, it matches photos where the physical build and facial structure is similar. He can change his appearance, but there are some things that he can't change without plastic surgery." Quentin's voice filled with elation. "This is a big step, Willow. Without your help, we wouldn't have gotten this far."

"Good. What about the guy with the metal teeth? Sounds like they have a last name for him."

"Yes, his last name is Vissor. He's a local thug that Mr. Smith must have shaken out of the bushes. He doesn't seem to know much. His communication was via third party and texting on a burner phone…at least that is what he says."

"That Scott guy figured out that you are more than a private citizen. What if he communicates that to Mr. Smith? Your cover will be blown."

"The locals can hold him for twenty-four hours for theft and harassment at the very least. After that, he might be able to make bail and communicate with Mr. Smith. My agency is working on trying to find a way to hold him longer."

The tightness in her stomach turned into a hard ball of nerves. "That could put you in even more danger and blow everything up."

Quentin tensed his jaw. "That means that this shoot might be my last chance to have the inside angle on Vertical Limit and maybe even draw Mr. Smith out."

Her heart pounded and she took in a deep breath. "We should get going then. I'm taking all my camera gear. I'm assuming we're not coming back here."

Quentin wiped his mouth with a napkin, picked up his plate and placed it in the dishwasher. "Hard to say. Far as I know this location is still safe for us. There was some guy driving by last night. The street ends in a cul-de-sac. He had to turn around. So clearly not someone who lived here." He pressed the buttons to start the dishwasher. "It could be nothing."

"I'll load up everything." What she hoped was that she could be back at her own home and swinging by to say hi to her mother before the day was over. Though that was probably pure fantasy on her part.

"Let me help you get the gear in the back of the car."

After everything was stowed in the back seat and the rest was in the trunk, they locked up the house and left.

The drive to Yellowstone was uneventful. Quentin explained the full plan to Willow as to where the backup would be. They found a parking space in the lot close to Old Faithful. This early in the season, the tourist traffic was just starting to grow.

"The Vertical Limit guy has your new number I assume," she said as she pushed open the door.

Quentin tapped the pocket where he kept his phone. "He should text us so we can find him."

"So glad I have my phone back."

She got out of the car before he did. She was wearing a light jacket and long-sleeve shirt, enough to keep out the spring chill. The early morning sun warmed her skin. Quentin rifled around in the back seat for the gun he'd stowed away.

The crowd on the boardwalk began to increase. Old Faithful must be due for an eruption soon. She preferred the less touristy parts of the park. Backcountry and remote areas of Yellowstone were some of her favorite places in the world.

Quentin came to stand beside her. A light breeze ruffled her hair. The sky was a crystal clear blue. It looked to be a great day to take some pictures of Trout Lake and the surrounding mountains…if that was all they did today.

He pulled his phone out, pressed buttons and then stared at the screen. He must have a text from the Vertical Limit guy. When she'd listened to the message from the scheduler, he had given the production coordinator's name as Calvin. She couldn't remember what his last name was. Quentin read the text and rubbed his five o'clock shadow. He drew his eyebrows together.

"What is it?"

"He just parked back behind the lodge. He said he got a little lost. I told him we'd drive over there and pick him up."

Why not meet in the parking lot they had agreed on? She stared out at Old Faithful as the geyser began to sputter and the crowd squeezed closer together. The lot by Old Faithful was nearly full, but there were still spaces to be found.

They climbed back into the car, and Quentin pulled out and drove toward the back side of the lodge where most of the employees parked. There were several cars but no people. A lean, dark-haired man got out of a compact car and waved.

"That must be him. I told him what kind of car I drove," Quentin said.

"I'll get out and sit in the back so you can make small talk with him and see if he gives anything up." Willow pushed open the door as the man approached.

Quentin got out as well. The man introduced himself as Calvin Ames. He shook hands with both Willow and Quentin. Willow couldn't get a clear read on him. Though he seemed a little nervous, he had a firm handshake and he had looked Willow in the eyes when he introduced himself.

"This is my first assignment," Calvin said once they were settled back in the car.

That might explain the nervousness. Willow sat in the back seat and hoped inexperience was why Calvin seemed a little on edge.

SIXTEEN

As he drove toward the trailhead, Quentin made small talk with Calvin in an attempt to gauge if this man truly was just a Vertical Limit employee or a plant sent to kill him and Willow. It bothered him that the location for meeting up had been changed at the last second. Dan's message had given a description of the car the agent would be in. Quentin hadn't had time to spot it in the lot. Hopefully, the guy was able to follow them to the location change and was behind them now.

Though Calvin was a new employee, it sounded like he had some experience in advertising and art.

From the back seat, Willow asked Calvin several questions about composition that he answered in a knowledgeable way. He appreciated the tag team approach in trying to assess where Calvin was coming from.

As they drove up a winding two-lane road, Quentin talked a little about the location they would be going to and his own experiences in Yellowstone. The sharing of personal stories was a technique designed to get Calvin to trust and maybe open up about his own life.

Calvin didn't take the bait and kept the conversation on a professional level.

"This would be a great location for aerial shots," Willow said. "We had a helicopter for our photo session up by Glacier Falls. I guess Vertical Limit didn't want to spring for it this time because of the accident that happened. I'm sure you heard about that."

Quentin didn't know if Willow's comment was calculated or just her trying to keep the conversation going, but it made Calvin twitch in his seat a little. A movement that was almost unnoticeable unless you were looking for it. Calvin cleared his throat. "No, I didn't hear anything."

Quentin suspected Calvin was lying. Even if he wasn't connected to Mr. Smith, he must have heard about the deaths. For about thirty seconds, Quentin listened to the car engine hum and the wheels roll across the asphalt.

"Guess that was before you came to work for Vertical Limit." There was an underlying waver to her voice. Only someone who knew her would have picked up on the fear.

As Quentin took a turn onto the road that led to the trailhead, a tightness spread through his chest. Even with backup, they'd be pretty isolated out here. He hoped they hadn't gotten in too deep.

Beyond being an assassin or a clueless employee, there was another possibility as to who Calvin was. He could be a plant Mr. Smith was grooming to become a courier. They did not know much about Mr. Smith's methods. Did he look for employees already working at Vertical Limit who were vulnerable to persuasion because of financial struggles as Henry had indicated, or did he recruit from the outside and then because of some unknown connection to Vertical Limit, he was able to get his henchmen hired there? Figuring out who Mr. Smith was would go a long way toward finding out what his connection to the company was. Getting someone to squeal on him would help even more.

They knew from the website that the Vertical Limit calendar was established six months ahead. That meant anyone could track where the company would be next. Mr. Smith could just plan his thefts around that. They knew for sure that anytime the stock photo company was in town, a theft had happened. The fencing of the items often coincided with the company working close by as well.

When Quentin pulled up to the trailhead, one other car was already parked on the flat dirt area. He wondered if that was his backup. There were several ways to get to the location. This hike was the most vigorous but also the fastest. The car could also belong to Mr. Smith or just to another hiker.

"If you guys don't mind. I've got my gear sorted into two backpacks, one bag with a shoulder strap and a tripod. I tried to keep it as simple and light as possible, but I will need some help with transport," Willow said.

"That's what I'm here for," said Quentin.

Once the equipment was unloaded, they each slipped into a backpack. Quentin grabbed the tripod and Calvin hauled the tote with the shoulder strap.

As he loaded up, Quentin watched Calvin lift his arms to slip into the backpack. He didn't see any bulge that would indicate Calvin had a gun. But he had to assume Calvin was armed if Quentin was going to keep him and Willow safe.

His memory of this hike was that the trail would become steep fairly quickly. The leaves on the trees were just beginning to bud and show some green.

"If you two want to step in, I'll take up the rear. The trail is pretty clearly marked." As the guide, he should probably be in front, but he needed to keep an eye on Calvin. Calvin being in front would be the safest for Willow and him.

Calvin narrowed his eyes but then shrugged.

They took off with Calvin in the lead and Willow in the middle keeping her distance from Calvin. She gave Quentin a nervous backward glance. Even before the trail grew steep and rocky his own heart was pounding.

They arrived at the location without passing any other hikers. This trail dead-ended at the top of a mountain that looked down on the lake. It didn't loop around.

Quentin looked around wondering where the backup agent was hidden.

After getting some direction from Calvin, Willow set up her tripod and then wandered around looking through her camera from different angles. The view on the plateau was breathtaking, a panoramic picture of the valley below, the lake and even some wildflowers in the distance. Quentin's attention was drawn to the sudden drop-off and the rocky ground below. He stepped back from the edge of the plateau.

Calvin watched him, as his eyes drew into snake-like slits. "Kind of steep."

"For sure," said Quentin.

Calvin's posture, squaring his shoulders and setting his jaw, held an unvoiced threat.

Nothing was for sure. Calvin hadn't yet tried to hurt them. Maybe he was just waiting for an opportunity.

And maybe Quentin and Willow had been running and under siege for so long that he was reading into the interaction things that weren't there.

On purpose, Quentin brought his shoulder blades together, so his unzipped jacket flipped open and the gun he had in a side holster was visible.

Calvin's whole demeanor changed. His body was like a balloon losing air as his jaw dropped. "Aren't those illegal in the park?"

Quentin shrugged. "No. The park allows them." He stepped toward Calvin, holding him in his gaze. "Lot of wild animals out here. I need to make sure the people with me are safe."

Willow must have picked up on the tension between the two men because she stopped taking pictures and turned in their direction. "Everything okay?"

Quentin hoped that the appearance of the gun would be enough to deter Calvin from whatever he might have planned. His guts told him Calvin was not an innocent employee. "Everything is just fine here, Willow." He turned in a circle watching the trees and waiting.

Calvin advanced toward Willow. "Let me have a look at the shots you have so far."

Willow glanced at Quentin as if trying to discern what was really going on. She clearly sensed something was up. He could not communicate with her in any meaningful way without Calvin noticing.

Calvin came to stand beside her, and she angled her camera so Calvin could see the shots she'd already taken. Again, she gave Quentin a quick look.

He could only shake his head in answer to the query he detected in her expression. Feeling on edge, he stepped toward them. "These are good," said Calvin.

He turned and faced where the mountain turned into a cliff. "I wonder if we can get some shots of the area in a way that is more panoramic."

"Sure, I can do that. I will have to switch out lenses to get all of that in." Willow retreated toward the edge of the cliff where she had put down the camera bag with the long strap.

Calvin stepped toward her.

Alarmed, Quentin quickened his pace toward them. It would take only a second for Calvin to push Willow off the steep precipice to her death. Would he do that and risk being shot? There were rocks he could use for cover, close enough that he could get behind them before Quentin had time to draw his weapon. The shock at seeing Quentin's gun had been genuine. Calvin had not counted on that.

Quentin kneeled by Willow at the same time Calvin did.

"Willow." Quentin was a little breathless. "Why don't you scoot away from the edge there?" He tried to make his voice sound casual. "Some of the footing around that precipice is more unstable than you may realize."

Willow looked up at him and then at Calvin. Maybe she had started to pick up on the emotional game of cat and mouse that was being played.

He studied the trees again remembering how well Mr. Smith and Yellowshirt had been hidden the last time. Then he glanced at Calvin. Every instinct and inch of his training told him something bad was going to happen.

Willow picked up her camera bag and scooted away from the precipice. Years ago, she and Quentin had hang glided off these cliffs. They were considered to be some of the most stable around. Unless there had been some erosion or an earthquake she hadn't heard about that had destabilized the area, Quentin's remark had been intended as a signal to her that things were not safe in a different way.

Her heart beat a little faster as she switched out her camera lenses. Her trembling hands made her fumble as she twisted the camera lens onto the body. Until Calvin made some sort of overt move, they had to continue this act.

She studied the thick undergrowth and trees that surrounded them. How long before Calvin tried something or someone burst through the trees?

In order to get the shot Calvin wanted, she was going to have to stand close to the edge. She rose and turned toward the precipice. She had to think fast. "Calvin, that backpack closest to you has a collapsible reflector disc in the main compartment. Can you grab it and hold it for me? It might help deflect some of the natural light, so we don't get random reflections. The sun is not exactly in an optimal spot."

The disc would do no such thing. It was designed to soften direct sunlight which, because of the overcast sky, they were not dealing with. She hoped that Calvin didn't know enough about photography to guess that she was just trying to make sure he wouldn't be able to push her over the edge with his hands full.

Once Calvin had flipped open the reflector disc, she instructed him to stand back and off to the side.

Calvin shifted his weight and looked out at the precipice. "Why doesn't Quentin hold this so I can see how you're framing the shots?"

If Quentin had to hold something, it would make it that much harder for him to grab his gun quickly or keep Calvin from pushing Willow over the edge. Willow glanced at the sky. "We probably should just get this done. Looks like there might be a thunderstorm moving in." She didn't wait for a reply. Instead she rose to her feet and moved toward where the mountain dropped off. "I'll show you the shots after I have taken all of them. It will be faster that way."

She was scrambling for an excuse to keep Calvin holding the disc and away from her. It seemed to have worked. Calvin did not voice an objection as she lifted the camera to her face.

Her hands were shaking as she framed her photo and clicked away, turning in a half circle as she did so. She was glad that her skill and experience allowed her to go on autopilot.

She aimed the camera downward to show the depth of the valley that led to the lake. Finally, she zoomed in on the lake in the distance, taking several shots of that as well.

She stepped away from the edge of the cliff and walked toward Calvin. She leaned close as she flipped through the digital shots she'd taken. "Is that what you want?" She gripped the camera tighter so Calvin wouldn't see her shaking hand.

Calvin took the camera in his hands and clicked through the photos slowly.

If he had been hired to kill both Quentin and her, Calvin certainly played the part of production coordinator well. Her guess was he would continue the theater act until he was sure he had an opportunity to eliminate both of them.

Calvin let out a heavy sigh and then glanced at Quentin, whose posture suggested he was a lion ready to pounce.

"I think we got what we need," said Calvin.

"Great. Let's pack up and get out of here. We probably have twenty minutes before that storm reaches us." Willow spoke as she kneeled on the ground and placed her camera safely in its case after removing the memory card.

Within minutes, they were ready to head back down the rocky trail. Something felt really off. If Calvin had been sent to kill them, this location was his best opportunity. Calvin's reaction indicated that he was surprised Quentin had a gun. Maybe that was what had made him not take action.

At Quentin's urging, Calvin walked in front. Though he didn't seem happy with the arrangement, he agreed. More than once, she caught Quentin glancing over his shoulder. Maybe looking for the backup that was supposed to be hiding at the location.

As they neared the trailhead, rain sprinkled out of the darkening sky. Lightning filled the sky. Thunder sounded in the distance.

They arrived at the car. The other car was still parked at the trailhead. The men put the gear on the ground. She opened the back door of the car, preparing to load her bags.

Quentin pulled his phone out and checked it.

Calvin checked his phone as well, stepping away from the car.

Willow loaded the gear into the back seat. She could see Quentin through the window as he read his text. He wandered toward the other parked car with his attention still on his phone.

Calvin had moved toward the bumper of their car. He was a few feet away facing her.

Willow picked up a backpack and placed it carefully on the seat.

She caught sight of Quentin as he peered into the back seat of the other parked car.

When he looked up at her, his face had drained of color and fear was etched across his features.

Willow felt razor-sharp edge of cold metal against her neck. Calvin spoke into her ear. "Don't move an inch or you'll die."

SEVENTEEN

When he saw the terror in Willow's expression, Quentin's heart squeezed tight.

Calvin stepped out from behind the open car door, dragging Willow with him. "Pull your gun and drop it on the ground or she gets it." With Quentin armed, Calvin had taken some time to find the opportunity he needed.

Calvin's whole countenance had changed. His eyes held a violent intensity that had been masked up to this point.

When Quentin had wandered over to the car, what he had seen in the back seat had caused what was happening to become crystal clear. There was a man lying in the back of the car maybe dead, maybe unconscious. No doubt, the backup agent. The change in location when they picked up Calvin had been intentional to throw off anyone who might try to follow them. Mr. Smith had not made an appearance, but he was pulling all the strings.

Quentin knew Calvin intended to kill them. The text that had been waiting for Quentin was from headquarters.

Good news and bad news. We have identified the man known only as Mr. Smith. Scott Vissor escaped custody.

That meant Scott had probably gotten in touch with

Mr. Smith and let him know his suspicions about Quentin. His cover was blown.

As his heart pounded in his chest, Quentin knew he needed to buy some time and wait for a moment of weakness or inattention. Not having the gun would seriously handicap him.

"I said pull the gun...slowly." Calvin jerked the knife so that his fist landed a blow against Willow's larynx.

She let out a gasp and then she sputtered for breath, wheezing and coughing.

Calvin commanded, "Take off your jacket so I can see what you're doing. Then keep one hand in the air while you pull the gun and toss it."

Thoughts tumbled through Quentin's mind at high speed. While he watched Calvin with his focus on what he was doing with the knife, Quentin registered everything in his peripheral vision, searching his surroundings for anything that might be used as a weapon or a way of escape.

Calvin had positioned himself behind Willow so that she served as a shield. Quentin could see only part of Calvin's face as he angled his head to watch Quentin.

Even if he managed to pull the gun and aim it, there was too much of a risk of missing and shooting Willow instead.

Quentin slipped out of his jacket. Cool spring air ruffled his cotton shirt. He knew one thing. If he didn't do something fast, he and Willow would die here. Their bodies might be dragged off the trail and not found for weeks.

"Drop the jacket now." Calvin's voice had taken on a nervous edge.

Not good. Fear could make Calvin even more impulsive.

Thunder sounded in the distance. Rain sprinkled down.

Willow looked right at him and raised her eyebrows. Communicating that she was about to do something?

She kicked Calvin in the shin. The move was not enough that he let go of her, but it stunned him, causing him to jerk the knife a few inches away from her throat.

There wasn't time to unsnap the security strap, pull the gun and aim. Quentin rushed toward the other two people. Willow had managed to twist free of Calvin's grasp.

Calvin lunged toward her with the knife. Willow dodged free of the trajectory of the blade but fell to her knees from the exertion. Quentin jumped into the fray and reached for Calvin's hand that held the weapon. Calvin stepped back holding the knife close to his body and pointing it at Quentin. The two men locked gazes but did not move.

Calvin started swinging the knife and advancing toward Quentin. Quentin reached to unsnap the security strap of his gun as he stepped back.

Off to the side, he heard the sound of a car engine roaring to life. Willow had gotten to her feet and started his car. The back door was still open where she'd been loading her gear. Calvin stalked toward Willow as she sat in the driver's seat of the car.

Quentin charged at Calvin, knocking him to the ground. Calvin had landed on his side but turned to face Quentin. Quentin reached for the knife. In the struggle, his hand touched the blade which sliced his palm. Pain surged through him.

With his uninjured hand, he landed a blow to Calvin's solar plexus, knocking the wind out of him. Quentin rose to his feet and jumped into the back seat while

Willow was backing up. He had to pull the door shut with his injured hand.

Willow had turned the car around. Calvin beat the back window with his fist twice before she was able to get up enough speed to get away from him.

"You all right?" Willow kept her focus on the rain-slicked road.

Quentin stared down at the bleeding gash on his palm. "I'll survive." Though the cut was not deep enough to require stitches, he was feeling a little light-headed.

"There's a small first-aid kit in the front pouch of the brown backpack," Willow said.

"Thanks." He took a moment to catch his breath before unzipping the pocket. "Sorry, some of your equipment got left behind. That was fast thinking back there."

He reached into the backpack and pulled out a plastic bag. He could see a condiment-sized packet of disinfectant and bandages.

The rainfall increased. As Willow angled into a curve, the car slid in the mud. She slowed down.

Quentin managed to squeeze some disinfectant gel on his cut.

"We might have trouble."

Quentin glanced out the back window. The car that had been parked at the trailhead was behind them.

The other car drew close enough for Quentin to make out Calvin behind the wheel. He prayed that the agent in the back seat wasn't dead. The road was so narrow it barely allowed two cars going in the opposite direction to pass.

Willow sped up but not by much. Quentin pulled his gun. His shooting hand was the one with the cut. He grabbed some gauze from Willow's first-aid kit and wrapped it around his hand. That would help some with the pain, but shooting was going to be a challenge.

The other car surged forward, hitting their back bumper.

The jarring motion caused him to bite his tongue. Willow let out a scream but kept her hands on the wheel and her eyes on the road. They were maybe ten minutes from the paved road where they could go much faster.

Quentin rested the gun on his thigh and held on to it loosely with his bandaged hand. When he glanced out the back window, the other vehicle was within a few feet of them. Close enough that Quentin could see Calvin's grimace.

Calvin's car surged forward, so they were side by side. Willow was forced to drift to the edge of the road.

Her voice filled with panic. "He's trying to push me off."

"Hold steady, Willow."

Calvin jerked the wheel and banged on the passenger side of Quentin's car. Their car vibrated from impact.

Willow eased away from Calvin's car. They were half on the road and half in the bank. She pressed the gas and turned the wheel to try to get back on the road and ahead of Calvin at the same time.

Calvin drifted over even more until Willow had to get off the road altogether or risk being slammed again.

The car rumbled and bumped over the rough terrain. There were trees up ahead. Willow managed to get around the first two before her back wheel started to spin in the mud.

"We're stuck."

"Ease off the gas and rock it back and forth."

"I know what to do." She shifted into Reverse.

Quentin glanced up. All he saw was the edge of the road. No sign of the other car. The path to get back on the road was not a clear one. To avoid the trees, they would have to go even farther down the side of the hill.

Despite Willow's careful maneuvering, the wheels kept spinning. Even if they did get unstuck, Calvin was probably waiting for them up on the road.

"Willow, we have to get out and run," Quentin said.

Willow shifted into Reverse and then back into Drive as the engine made grinding sounds. "I can get us out of here."

"Maybe, if we had time." He glanced up at the road, catching a view of Calvin staring down at them. Quentin shook Willow's arm and then pointed up the hill.

She stopped pressing the gas and turned off the engine.

As they piled out of the car, Quentin looked over his shoulder. Calvin was advancing toward them. Quentin pulled his gun and shot knowing that the bullet would fall short of its target but hoping it was enough to warn off or slow Calvin. Pain zinged through his cut palm where he gripped the gun.

As they hurried toward the cover of the trees, Quentin again gazed up at their pursuer retreating back up to the road. That meant he was most likely going to drive down and try to catch them when they got to the main road.

The brush and the trees grew thicker as they ran down the incline. Once they were deep into the forest and hidden by the trees, they slowed down.

"My guess is…he's going to be looking for us…at the intersection." She sucked in a ragged breath. "Assuming we would follow the road down."

He nodded. "He didn't want to come after us because of my gun. That means we'll have to come out a ways from there." The intersection formed a T so there was only the choice of going east or west once you made it to the base of the mountain.

"Guess we got a little bit of a hike ahead of us," she said.

It started to rain again as they worked their way through the trees in the general direction of the road. Quentin remembered the text he'd received. Dan had also said he had news concerning what the forensic accountant had learned about Vertical Limit but would give him the details later. They had a name to go with Mr. Smith. They were getting so close which might mean Mr. Smith would become much more desperate. And now he probably knew that Quentin was undercover and that Quentin knew of Mr. Smith's connection to Vertical Limit.

Without a jacket, Quentin's clothes quickly became soaked. Willow walked ahead of him a few feet. He checked his phone which had a signal. Once they made it to the road, they could call a park ranger to come and get them. As it was there was no way he could even give an approximate location to the ranger.

They walked for what felt like a long time though maybe the cold made time move more slowly. Still they did not hear or see any sign that they were getting closer to the road. The forest had become thicker and more overgrown. He started to lose hope that they would get back to civilization and that the case against Mr. Smith would ever be closed.

Shivering he walked a little faster to catch up with Willow. She stared ahead deep in thought. Looking down only when the terrain became dicey. He'd always known she was a good person, but now he knew she had an iron will and problem-solving skills any agent would be glad to have.

"We made a good team back there getting away from Calvin. Thank you for thinking quick and getting to the car."

She took a few steps before answering. "I always thought we made a good team."

"Me too." He listened to the squishing sound his hiking boots made as they traversed a muddy patch of ground. "I always thought we were good together too. I don't know why things fell apart."

She slowed her pace. "Why do we have to go over this? Luke died. It was too much for either of us to bear."

"What if we had made different choices? What if we had been there for each other?"

She stopped and turned to face him. "The point is, that is not what happened. You left me."

Rain trickled down the side of his face. The cold had soaked through his skin. He knew he needed to say what had been on his mind almost from the moment he'd looked up and saw Willow in that helicopter. Speaking the truth might destroy the fragile bond between them. "I felt like you drove me away when you said you didn't love me anymore."

Her words came out in almost a whisper. "I guess there is plenty of blame to go around."

The softness of her response made him lean closer to her. "Look if…when I wrap this case up, I intend to move back to Little Horse. Could we at least give friendship a shot?"

Her eyes searched his. "If all this proves nothing else,

our time together shows we can look out for each other. I suppose we could manage a friendship."

Even though he was chilled to the bone, her words and her smiled warmed him.

She stared out at the trees in front of her. "Kind of a moot point right now though, isn't it?"

"What do you mean?"

"We're a long way from being able to catch your Mr. Smith."

It wasn't looking good for them either way. The news that an undercover agent had gotten so close to Mr. Smith might send him into hiding. The only thing that would keep him out in the open was that he'd made it clear he wanted Quentin and Willow dead.

The conversation with Quentin still echoed in her mind as Willow turned and continued to walk. It seemed like they should have come to the road by now or at least seen signs that they were getting closer. There was no echo of cars rumbling by on the paved road to indicate they were anywhere close.

She wondered if they had somehow gotten turned around and were headed deeper into the forest than back to the more populated part of the park.

Everything felt so upside down and uncertain. If Mr. Smith wasn't captured, she might have to leave Little Horse forever. If he was arrested, Quentin would be moving back to Little Horse.

The rain had soaked through her clothes.

Quentin pulled his phone out. "I have a signal. What if we call for help? The nearest ranger station should be able to send someone to search for us."

"Quentin, we don't even know where we are."

Willow took in her surroundings, not seeing any obvious place to take shelter. The trees were just starting to bud and would not keep the rain out.

"Maybe we could get back to the car and take shelter there." Quentin was shivering so badly his voice vibrated.

That was at least twenty minutes uphill. "Just off the road like that, we'd be easier to locate for sure. They'd be able to come for us quickly."

She listened to the rain. Neither one of them said what they were both probably thinking. What if Calvin went back looking for them at the car when they didn't show up at the crossroads?

They couldn't stay out here much longer.

There was no good choice here.

He took his phone out. "I'm going to call for help. I'll let them know we're headed back toward the car. They can locate it fast because it's close to the road. They might be waiting for us by the time we get there."

She nodded. "It seems the smarter thing to go back to a location we know can be found than to hope we run into help up ahead." The road leading up to the lake had no mile markers. "I think we were more than halfway down the mountain when we got stuck."

He wiped the water off his face. The phone was getting soaked. She tore her jacket off and stepped toward him. She used the coat as a shield over the phone. "So you can at least see the screen."

"Thanks." He entered the number and explained the situation. Quentin must have had the phone on speaker because she could hear the operator promise to send someone to that area as quickly as possible.

They trudged back up the mountain toward where

the car was. The ground had become slicker from the rain which was coming down in sheets. They huddled closer together and forged ahead.

Though it felt like an eternity, eventually they came through the trees and could locate the car still stuck in the mud. The overcast sky had caused it to feel more like nighttime.

They increased their pace. She didn't see any signs of another car on the road up above. The sound of the rain altered and then she felt the needle sting of hail hitting her skin. The change made them move even faster.

Both of them were beyond freezing when they were within feet of the car.

"You get in," Quentin said. "I think I have some emergency provisions in my trunk."

Willow reached out for the cold metal of the door handle and dragged herself inside. She crossed her arms and rocked trying to get warm. She had a vague awareness that Quentin had opened the driver's side door to push the button that released the trunk latch.

Her focus and ability to register her surroundings had become fuzzy. Hypothermia must be setting in. The shivering meant she was still in the early stages. Quentin must be in even worse shape. He'd been without a jacket. Quentin opened the front driver's side door and turned the engine on. A moment later, she felt a blast of heat.

He crawled in beside her, placing a space blanket over her shoulders. "Need to get your core warm," he said.

"My hands are so cold."

"That's an easy thing to fix." He placed a warm square packet in each of her hands. Relishing the heat, she pressed her hands together and drew them toward her chest. He leaned close to her and draped a blanket over his shoulders and also around her. "Are you okay with me being this close?"

Despite the direness of their situation, she laughed. "It's just for warmth, right?"

Quentin didn't answer but put his arm around her back and drew her close. They huddled together while the hail pinged on the metal of the car.

Gradually, the shivering stopped. The hail came down so fast that it covered much of the windshield.

Willow closed her eyes and turned her head to rest on Quentin's chest. She found comfort in his arms. She'd missed this.

Quentin stirred. She opened her eyes. "What is it?"

The hail blocked most of the view through the windshield.

"I'm not sure, but I think I saw flashing lights."

Willow took in a breath and turned to gaze out the side window. She tilted her head to see up toward the road they had slid off. "I don't see anything."

"Maybe I should get out." Quentin moved away from her. "I don't want the ranger to miss us."

She still did not see any light. "If it is the ranger…" She knew there was a chance Calvin would come back looking for them.

EIGHTEEN

Quentin had seen only a flash of light and then it was gone. It could have been a car going by and it could have been Calvin.

He clicked on the windshield wipers to clear the hail off, stared out at the darkness and then turned on the headlights. Maybe he had just imagined seeing light.

Willow leaned forward. Her hand touched his headrest as she searched as well. She scooted across the seat and stared out the side window to have a view of the road.

"See anything?"

"No," she said.

"I'm going to get out. He may have driven past. When he doesn't find us, he'll turn back around. I don't want him to miss us on the way down."

"Wouldn't the 911 dispatcher have passed on your phone number? Why doesn't he just call us?"

He pulled his phone out and stared at the black screen. "The battery is dead."

"Quentin, we just got warmed up. I don't think going out in the cold is such a good idea."

He had to say what both of them were probably assuming. "Are you thinking it could just be Calvin up there looking for us?"

"Of course that has crossed my mind."

"Maybe the headlights will be enough for us to be seen." He pulled his revolver from the holster and checked the cylinder. Three bullets left. He put the gun on the console.

The windshield wipers swished back and forth. The hail had turned to sleet and was swirling in the headlights. This early in the spring it wasn't unusual to get sleet or even snow. The temperature must have dropped.

The car had become toasty warm.

Ten minutes passed. He began to question if he had even seen lights flash.

"There." Willow pointed toward the road. "Someone is up there."

The leather seat creaked as Quentin reached for the gun and peered up at where Willow had indicated. He saw it as well. A car must have stopped above them.

Willow whirled around to stare out the back window. "He's coming this way."

The glowing circle of a flashlight wobbled toward them.

"You stay inside. Let me get out and talk to the guy." He gripped the gun, pushed open the door and stepped outside ready for whatever he was facing. The cold wind and hail stabbed at his skin.

The light bobbed up and down as it came closer. He could see only the man's silhouette. The man stopped when he was about twenty feet away and pointed the light toward Quentin.

"I understand you folks are stranded."

Quentin squinted and jerked his head back to get out of the direct path of the light. He breathed a sigh of relief. The voice was unfamiliar. "Yes. There are two of us." He opened the back door and spoke to Willow. "It's all clear."

Within minutes, he had grabbed Willow's bag and a backpack of camera gear, and they were in the ranger's warm vehicle. Quentin sat up front while Willow got in the back with her camera gear.

Both of them were so beyond tired that the ranger did most of the talking. He introduced himself as Rolf. "Lot of rain coming down pretty fast. Got a little bit of flooding in parts of the park. If you don't mind, I'll drop you two off at my cabin. I got some other calls to go out on."

"That would be fine," Quentin answered.

"Probably won't be able to get a tow truck up to pull your car out until tomorrow."

When they arrived at the cabin, the ranger told them to make themselves at home. "Eat whatever you like. There's plenty of dry firewood." After unlocking the door for them, the ranger drove away through the storm.

They stepped inside the cabin which was one large room with a ladder leading to a loft. A door off to the side must be where the bathroom was.

Quentin put down the backpack he had carried for Willow. "What is our priority here? Getting dried off or eating?" His clothes were already partially dry from his having sat in the warm car.

"Can't we do both? I'll see what I can find in the kitchen if you want to start a fire. We can sit in front of it to dry off."

The cabin was chilly which meant the woodstove must be the primary heat source. He found dry wood on the covered back porch underneath a tarp. By the time Quentin got the woodstove going, Willow brought him a steaming bowl of chili.

She set another plate with crackers on it down on the coffee table in front of the two easy chairs that faced the woodstove. Willow returned with another steaming bowl and sat down in the other chair.

He ate slowly. The house warmed up as did his stomach. Willow finished her bowl and set it on the coffee table. She sat back in the chair and closed her eyes. Her breathing changed, indicating that she had fallen asleep. Though it was early evening, it was clear the trauma of the day had taken its toll.

Quentin got up and pulled his phone out. He had noticed a charger on a table by the back door. He was grateful when he saw that it fit his phone. He plugged his phone in and stared out at the sleet coming down and the drizzle on the window.

After finding a throw to cover Willow, he plunked down in the other easy chair. She looked really beautiful when she slept. He had to catch himself when out of habit he wanted to reach over and brush the hair off her face. Her strawberry blonde hair always got curlier when it got wet.

He took in a deep breath trying to quell the rising sense of despair. He had a phone call to make to his supervisor, but he was sure that now that his cover was blown it meant he'd be pulled out of his undercover assignment. To what degree he would be involved in the investigation was uncertain…if at all.

This might be the end of the line for him. David Stone's death would be in vain. David, who was fifteen years older than Quentin and thinking of retiring or at least moving to a desk assignment, had left behind a wife and three kids. David had not only shown Quentin the ropes working undercover but had been the one who had helped Quentin forgive himself over what had happened to Luke.

He rested his tensed hands on the arms of the easy chair and focused on the comforting crackle of the wood burning and the flames in the window of the woodstove until he was able to relax. His muscles were as fatigued as his mind. He needed to rest.

His supervisor had said something about tracking down the owner of Vertical Limit. Maybe that would provide a lead.

He said a prayer knowing that whatever happened, God was in control.

With Mr. Smith still at large and probably getting ready to lie low, Willow would have to be put in witness protection. Quentin glanced over at her as she turned her head to the side and pulled the blanket around her shoulders.

He dreaded giving her that news.

Willow awoke in darkness to the noise of Quentin snoring in the chair next to her. The fire had become glowing embers though the cabin remained toasty warm. She heard a strange buzzing that her groggy state did not quite register. The noise was coming from the kitchen. When she looked in that direction a phone glowed on the counter.

She rose with the blanket still wrapped around her shoulders. A text message from Calvin had just come up on the phone.

I know where you are.

Her heart thudded. She pulled the phone from the charger and hurried to wake Quentin. Because it was dark and she was unfamiliar with the room, she crashed into a plastic bucket that had been left by the counter. It fell on its side and rolled across the floor.

The noise was enough to cause Quentin to jump to his feet. "What?"

After commanding the flashlight feature on the phone to turn on, she hurried toward Quentin and showed him the text.

"What does it mean? Why is he warning us like that?" When she tried the lamp beside one of the easy chairs, it did not turn on. The electricity might be out, or it was run on a generator that shut down during nonpeak hours.

"Flashlight off," Quentin commanded.

Quentin did not answer her question but instead rushed toward the window that looked out on the gravel drive that connected to the road. He ran a patrol around the entire cabin, peering out each window and even opening the door and stepping outside.

He returned, closed the door and clicked the dead bolt. The door had previously been unlocked. They'd both been too tired to think about security. "I don't see anything out there. He might be trying to flush us out."

"But how could he even know we were here? Do you think he's bluffing to keep us afraid?"

Quentin paced and stared at his phone. His gaze fell on the two bags of photo gear Willow had managed to save. "Look through your bag for anything you didn't put in there. I'll take the backpack. He may have put a tracking device in there when we abandoned the car, knowing that you valued that equipment enough to come back for it." He turned his flashlight back on.

Willow dropped to the floor and started to search the pocket of the bag that held her favorite camera. She took the camera out and felt around. The flashlight was placed between the two bags, so it didn't fully illuminate where she was searching.

"Found it," Quentin said. "Hold the light for me. If I turn this off, he's going to know we found it."

"Should we call for help?"

"We can't stay here." Quentin placed the device on the end table by one of the easy chairs. "He's just waiting for his chance."

"But why warn us? He wants us to come out to try to run."

Quentin ran his hands through his hair. "If it's just him out there, he can't keep eyes on every part of the cabin. You call for help. I'm going to slip outside and toss this thing so it looks like we've left the cabin."

Willow doubted there were very many rangers on shift at this hour. And those who were working were probably dealing with the flooding issue the ranger who had found them had mentioned. How long would it take for help to show up?

Quentin moved around in the dark. He grabbed a coat that was hung on a hook. He opened the door only a sliver and stepped out into the cold dark night.

Willow's fingers were shaking as she dialed 911 and explained the situation to the operator.

"Which ranger cabin are you at?"

Willow had to think. Had the ranger said his name? "It is the one not too far from the road leading up to Trout Lake where the road T's off." She tried to recall the conversation between Quentin and the ranger as he drove them. "I think the ranger's name was Ralph or Wolf or something like that."

"Rolf," said the operator. "I know where you are. Can you sit tight until help can get there?"

"I can't answer that. I don't know if the man who sent the threatening text is close by or just trying to scare us."

"We'll get help out there as quickly as we can."

Willow said thank you and hung up. Realizing the glow of the phone might tell Calvin where she was, she put the phone in her pocket. She sat down low on the floor by one of the easy chairs. Her own phone had been in one of the camera bags they'd left behind.

The cabin made creaking noises as she listened to the sound of her own breathing. She tried not to give in to the fear that played around the edges of her emotions. She had to stay calm and alert.

Quentin should be back by now. How far did he intend to go with the tracker? He'd borrowed one of the ranger's coats, but it was still raining. He couldn't stay out there for long without getting cold all over again.

She waited a few more minutes and then crawled across the floor, pulled the curtain back a few inches and peered out. There was a porch light that must run on a battery. Still, she didn't see anything or anyone, no movement at all.

She settled back down by the chair.

A noise outside on the porch caused her to jump. She waited for Quentin to open the door just a sliver and squeeze back inside. The minutes ticked by as the silence fell around her like a heavy blanket.

Maybe an animal, a raccoon or possum, had climbed on the porch and knocked something down.

What was taking Quentin so long?

NINETEEN

Quentin kneeled down in the darkness partially hidden by some rocks. He watched the area where he'd placed the tracker hoping it would lure Calvin out so he could surprise him, hold him at gunpoint and march him back to the house where the rangers could take him into custody. He had been out in the rain long enough that he was starting to feel chilled again.

He surveyed each quadrant that surrounded him, turning nearly in a full circle and tuning his ears to any sound that might be out of place.

He rose to his feet and turned to face the cabin.

It was on fire. Flames shot out from the wood pile and licked at the door.

A force like a wall of bricks knocked him to the ground. In the darkness, he dropped the gun he'd been holding.

A tremendous weight rested on his chest while a fist pummeled his head. The body slam had knocked the wind out of him and disoriented him. Willow was probably still inside the cabin. He had to get his bearings and fast. He reached up pushing the chin of his assailant upward with force.

The move caused the weight on his chest to shift enough that Quentin had a little more leverage. He blocked the next attempted blow to his head and then threw the man off him.

It was hard to gauge where the man had landed in the dark. Quentin reached toward where he thought the man was. His hand grazed muscle, but the man dodged away.

In his peripheral vision, Quentin could see the flames consuming the cabin where Willow was. The fire was no accident. Hopefully Willow had escaped, but he couldn't count on that. He needed to find her.

The assailant, whom he assumed was Calvin, came after him again. This time Quentin was ready. He disabled the man with several blows to the stomach and head.

He leaned close to the body to make sure the unconscious man was still alive. Now he could make out some of the man's features. It wasn't Calvin. This was the man who had been with Mr. Smith at the falls. The man in the yellow shirt.

Quentin's blood froze. Mr. Smith had sent in reinforcements to make sure he and Willow didn't escape this time.

He ran back toward the cabin. The fire surrounded the entire perimeter. Someone had pushed a log splitter by the door so it would be impossible to open. Willow was trapped inside. He was grateful the rain had slowed the spread of the flames. He pushed the heavy log splitter out of the way. The doorknob was hot. Now he saw the broken window where fiery rags had been tossed in. There was smoke and fire inside the cabin as well.

He slipped out of his coat and wrapped it around the doorknob. As he pushed the door open someone grabbed him from behind. An arm wrapped around his neck and yanked him backward.

Quentin fell off the porch with the man as they wrestled. This wasn't Yellowshirt. It was Calvin. Quentin managed to get to his feet as did Calvin. Quentin lunged at Calvin, clamped his hand on the back of his neck and slammed his head against the porch railing. Calvin crumpled to the ground.

The interior of the cabin was smoky. Quentin picked up the wet jacket and put it over his nose and mouth as he dropped to the ground and crawled inside. With the darkness and the smoke, he couldn't see anything. He heard coughing and crawled toward it. He found Willow by swinging his hand out in front of him until it touched the fabric of her shirt.

She leaned toward him still coughing. She was only partially conscious. He half dragged, half carried her to the door. Flames surrounded the porch, and he could see Calvin's prone body as he lay on his side in the mud.

Willow was on her feet but bent over and wheezing. He wrapped his arm around her to guide her. As they made their way down the stairs, he could feel the heat from the flames.

Calvin stirred, groaning in pain. It was probably just a matter of minutes before Yellowshirt regained consciousness as well.

They weren't safe yet. Still helping Willow walk, he made his way to the side of the cabin that faced the road. He glanced up and down the road hoping to see a vehicle. He had no idea what response time in the park was like.

"You were able to call for help?"

"Yes." Willow coughed. "They will send someone

as soon as possible. The flood has made them short handed."

Though the cabin was remote, someone might see the flames and call that in as well.

What he knew right now was they could not count on help. He searched for a hiding place then directed Willow toward a cluster of trees. A shot was fired behind them.

Willow jerked away from him and stumbled. Fearing she'd been hit, his heart lurched. He reached for her and wrapped his arms around her. She was like a rag doll in his arms.

"Are you hit?"

She didn't answer. He continued to drag her toward the trees.

Had the men managed to find his gun, or had they brought one of their own? He couldn't count on there being only two bullets left in his gun if they had brought more fire power.

Because the trees were deciduous and just starting to bud, they would not provide much cover if the two men came looking with flashlights. The best thing would be to keep moving which meant they might miss the ranger when he showed up.

They moved deeper into the forest. He could hear noises that indicated at least one of the men had followed them.

Willow seemed to regain some of her strength. She straightened up. He let go of her waist. She must have just been shocked by the gunshot but not hit.

After they had been moving for a few minutes, Quentin stood still then dropped to the ground. Willow scooted in beside him. He didn't hear any noise to indicate the pursuer had been able to track them.

The smell of smoke in the air was still very strong even though they were some distance from the cabin.

Willow emitted a muffled cough that she tried to conceal.

He froze, hoping the sound did not alert their pursuer to their position.

Illumination from a flashlight glinted through the trees and edged toward them.

To run would ensure that they would be heard and spotted. Both of them remained motionless as the light passed over them and the pursuer moved toward something else that interested him, disappearing deeper into the trees.

After several minutes passed, the pursuer was no longer visible. Quentin searched the trees for the glow from the flashlight but saw nothing. The man had traveled far enough away that is was safe for them to move without risking detection. Quentin tugged on Willow's sleeve.

He led Willow in an arc through the trees that would get them closer to the cabin. He hoped to find a place where they could watch for the ranger when he came up the road. If fire trucks were called, the sound of the sirens might cause the two assailants to flee, but he couldn't count on that.

Quentin worried that if only a single ranger showed up to help them, he might be shot.

They settled into a place where the brush was a little thicker and they had a partial view of the road and the smoldering cabin. The rain seemed to have put out much of the fire. Which meant the fire department might not be called at all until the ranger got there and saw what was happening.

Quentin thought he saw movement around the cabin but couldn't be sure. He prayed there would be an opportunity to step out and warn the ranger before either he or Willow was shot at.

Willow spoke in a whisper. "Sorry about coughing back there. I must have breathed in a lot of smoke."

"You were half-unconscious when I found you."

"I could have died." Her voice took on a faraway quality as the realization sank in.

The two men must have parked a car somewhere. It was no place obvious, maybe back in the trees on the other side of the cabin.

Quentin craned his neck and then looked off to the side, not seeing any light or movement. They huddled together listening to the drizzle of the rain.

He turned his face toward her in the darkness. She looked at him as well.

"I thought you had been shot back there." He kept his voice soft. "That scared me."

Her hand covered his. "Sorry. The bullet came so close to me all I could hear was a ringing in my ears."

The silky smoothness of her hand covering his sent a charge of electricity through him despite the wet and cold.

"I don't want to think about a world without you in it."

She leaned close enough to him that he felt her breath on his neck when she spoke. "That's a really nice thing to say."

In that moment he wanted to kiss her, but he knew it was wrong.

Even before the words came out of his mouth, he realized what an empty thing it was to do. Once they got back to civilization, Willow would have to be put under some kind of protection. It was the only way to keep her safe. He'd never see her again.

In the darkness, Willow couldn't discern Quentin's eyes or expression clearly enough to read them. His voice had become husky, and his body language seemed to indicate that he might kiss her. Yet, he'd pulled back.

Maybe it was for the best. Even though she felt drawn to him in that moment, thinking that there could ever be anything romantic between them was probably not a good idea. He had saved her life back at the cabin. No doubt that was the source of the attraction, feeling safe with him, knowing he would protect her. All she had to do was not fan the flames of that emotion. Just let it go.

Willow stared out at the road. What was taking the ranger so long to show up? Certainly the operator had communicated the level of danger she and Quentin were in.

She lifted her head trying to see a little farther down the road.

Several minutes passed and then she saw the pin-holes of light still quite far away. The road dead-ended after the cabin. That had to be someone coming here.

Quentin touched her arm. "You need to stay put. Trust me, those guys are still hanging around looking for their chance."

The headlights drew closer. Willow tensed as her stomach did a somersault. What if it wasn't even the ranger coming to help them, but Mr. Smith coming to finish the job?

"Once we're sure it's the ranger, I'll signal to him. We'll make a run for it." He turned slightly to look off to the side and then behind him.

They had no idea where either of the two men were hiding.

The car drew closer and then Willow saw that there was a second car behind the first with a law enforcement insignia.

"Stay low and run fast," Quentin advised.

They sprinted toward the cars even before they had come to a full stop.

A shot was fired at them from behind. And then another shot came from by the cabin aimed at one of the police vehicles. A man and a woman got out of each of the cars, took cover behind their vehicles and pulled their weapons. The man fired two rounds toward the cabin. The female officer drew her attention to Quentin and Willow, pointing her gun toward them.

Quentin put his hands up. "We're unarmed. We're the ones who called."

The woman spoke in a loud and commanding voice. "Keep your hands where I can see them. Walk toward me."

"There is a danger we could be shot at," Willow said as she glanced over her shoulder. She crouched down while still keeping her hands in the air.

The female officer didn't answer right away. She kept her gun aimed at them. "Then get over here quickly and into the back of the vehicle."

Willow and Quentin sprinted the remaining distance. As they ran, Willow thought she heard a car starting up somewhere but couldn't be sure. They got into the back seat.

Willow watched as the ranger and the sheriff remained on guard with their guns drawn for several minutes before exchanging words. Both got into their vehicles. The female officer sat behind the wheel of the sheriff's car. She glanced in the rearview mirror.

"You folks doing okay?"

They nodded.

She turned the key in the ignition. "I'll be anxious to find out what went down here tonight. Rolf is not going to be happy about his cabin."

The radio started to squawk as calls went back and forth. A fire truck was being sent out to the cabin. The ranger said something about looking for the people who had shot at them, but Willow had a feeling they wouldn't be found.

The sheriff drove down the dark road. "I happened to be fairly close to the park when your call came in. It sounded like they might need some backup. The road to get here was flooded. We had to do a big circumnavigation."

That explained the delay in their showing up.

The steady hum of the car as it rolled down the road helped calm Willow down. They arrived at a ranger station where the sheriff took their statements. Not knowing how much Quentin would say about the depth of the investigation he was involved in, she stuck to the narrative that she was a freelance photographer hired by a company and that Calvin had attacked them both up at the shoot and then with some help at the cabin had come after them again.

Willow sat in the room that served as an interview room, though judging from the bulletin board and coffee maker it was also a break room for the rangers.

Feeling exhausted, she rested her head on the table. A knock on the door caused her to jerk.

Quentin stuck his head in. "They made arrangements to give us a ride. My car will be towed when it stops raining."

"I didn't tell them anything about your investigation."

"There is no reason for them to know."

"Where are we going?"

He stepped into the room and closed the door, leaning against it. "The safe house in Helena is still secure. We'll stay there for the night."

She noticed dread or maybe fear in Quentin's voice and expression. "And then what?"

"With my cover blown, I'll be pulled out of the field. I'm not sure in what capacity I will be involved with the investigation…maybe none."

Quentin's tone was one of complete and utter defeat.

"I'm so sorry after you got so close to catching Mr. Smith."

Quentin swallowed, causing his Adam's apple to move up and down. He stared at the floor for a moment before looking her in the eye. "Willow, I have to tell you. With Mr. Smith still at large, you may have to stay in a temporary safe house until he is caught and brought to trial."

Willow pushed the chair back and rose to her feet. "And if he isn't caught?" Her throat went tight.

"He's just too dangerous. If we can get you a deal to testify once he's caught, you might be able to go into witness protection."

Willow felt like she'd been punched in the stomach and hit in the head. Her vision blurred and she realized she was crying. She shook her head, but no words came. This possibility had loomed over her since the beginning. She had believed though that if she fought hard enough and helped Quentin with the investigation, it wouldn't happen.

Quentin took a step toward her and gathered her into his arms. "I'm so sorry."

Her whole world was about to be ripped away from her. "Will I even be able to say goodbye to my mother?"

He brushed his palm over her hair. "We'll try to make that happen."

Silent tears fell while Quentin held her. Being in his arms was a comfort. Just when they seemed to be mending the chasm between them, she would be yanked away forever.

"More than anything, I'm sorry you got dragged into this," Quentin said.

She pulled back and looked into his eyes. He was a good man with a strong sense of justice who always tried to do the right thing. "I don't blame you. Please don't think that."

His eyes searched hers. Her lips parted as she stared into his blue eyes. He leaned down. His lips touched hers. As he deepened the kiss, a photo album of memories, times they had shared, both good and bad, flooded her mind.

He pulled back and rested his hand on her cheek. His eyes were glazed with tears as well.

The kiss was what she had wanted even though she knew it was a goodbye kiss.

TWENTY

Once Quentin cleared it with Special Agent Linman, he and Willow were given the thumbs-up to stay at the safe house in Helena. He still needed to call his supervisor and get the details that had been discovered about Vertical Limit and what Mr. Smith's real name was. A sheriff's deputy offered to give them a ride.

Quentin sat in the front seat with the deputy.

Both he and Willow nodded off once they were on the highway.

Quentin woke. Still a bit groggy, he watched the broken yellow lines of the highway clip by, knowing that within twenty-four hours Willow would be lost to him, probably forever. Their time together, despite all the drama, had made him realize how big the hole in his life was without her. Though he'd been running away from his pain for five years, he was ready to come home, but it would be without Willow there as a friend.

The kiss had reminded him that they had once shared a deep connection. The gash in his heart made him think he would not ever get into a relationship again. Willow really had been his first and only love.

Maybe he'd have to give up on catching Mr. Smith.

The man had probably gone deep underground by now. He could live his life taking care of his father and the ranch. Maybe go back to school and become a history teacher, something he had dreamed of doing.

None of those plans made him feel any better. He nodded off for a while longer, resting his head against the window. When he woke up again, they were five miles from Helena.

Classical music on a low volume floated out of the car speakers. Willow had lain down in the back seat and was still fast asleep.

Quentin was too tired and too distraught to try to make small talk with the deputy. He watched the billboards for restaurants and hotels as the headlights brought them into view. Willow stirred when the car got into town and slowed down.

"Which way?" asked the deputy.

Quentin gave him directions as they rolled through the dark residential streets. Once they came to the house, the deputy pulled into the driveway by the garage. The street was totally quiet at this hour. He did notice a curtain being pulled back on a second-story window across the street.

Though he'd slept for part of the journey, he had checked to see if they were being followed.

Quentin opened the back door and shook Willow's shoulder. "We're here."

Once Willow was on her feet, he thanked the deputy. The red taillights of the car disappeared around a corner, and he and Willow made their way to the door. Quentin unlocked it, and they stepped inside the dark room.

Willow turned on one light, enough to see by. She

pulled Quentin's phone out of her pocket and handed it to him. She headed up the stairs. She walked like she was still half asleep. Quentin made sure the doors were locked. He peered out of all the ground floor windows, not seeing any signs of life, cars or lights. Hopefully the place was still secure.

He had a text from his supervisor saying to call him. Even at this hour?

Quentin pressed in the number.

His supervisor answered right away. Judging from the energy in his voice he had not awakened him. That meant the case was still hot enough that headquarters was pursuing it with gusto and not bothering to sleep. So much of what the agency did involved sitting in an office at a computer and communicating with other agencies, local and federal. Quentin had always preferred the action-oriented part of the job, but all that would be changing.

"Hey, Quentin. How are you doing?"

"Tired, and I don't mean just physically."

"I get that," said Dan. "First the good news is that the locals picked up Calvin. We'll pull his sheet and figure out what his connections are, but I suspect he's just another hired thug."

"No sign of the other guy who was with Mr. Smith?"

"No, he has vanished."

"When I saw him up at the falls his face was familiar from the surveillance photos we had. I think his connection to Mr. Smith runs deeper than most."

"We suspect he's Mr. Smith's right-hand man," Dan said.

"You don't have to tell me the bad news. I know what

is coming. Willow will have to be put in a safe house, and I'll be pulled out of the field."

"Don't lose heart, Quentin. What you say is true, but what Willow was able to do with the artist sketch has given us a name and a face. We were able to scan surveillance footage of the places where items were stolen. We have reason to believe that Mr. Smith's real name is Kirk Simonson. We're going to catch him."

Right now, he didn't want to think about the investigation. His only focus was to make sure he got Willow to a place where she would be safe.

"On top of that, we've had our forensic accountant working on tracking down the owner of Vertical Limit. The true owner has covered his tracks, but we suspect the company was set up under one of Kirk's other identities or using one of his associates as a front."

"All of that is good news," said Quentin. "Now that Mr. Smith, Kirk, knows how close we were to getting him with my cover being blown, I'm sure he will go underground."

"It might take a year or more. We don't know what his funds and resources are, but Kirk Simonson has a compulsion to steal. He'll reinvent himself and surface again sooner or later. Even if the investigation goes dormant for a while, we've got so much intel on him right now that catching him will be that much easier."

Maybe he should just take the retirement he had planned and let someone else in the agency work this case, especially if they had to wait a year for another lead to pop up. It would mean that he wouldn't feel a sense of closure over David Stone's death.

"We have Willow to thank for all that we've been

able to uncover. It has come at a tremendous personal cost to her."

Dan didn't answer right away. "I get that. We'll be working through the night to set up a new safe house and then a new identity for her."

"She really wants the chance to say goodbye to her mother. That is the only family she has left." He took in a sharp breath. "Her brother died five years ago."

"I can't make any promises. We'll do our best."

Quentin hung up. He didn't even bother going upstairs to sleep. Instead he grabbed a throw and lay down on the couch.

Hours later, he awoke to the smell of coffee. Willow was up and dressed in a shirt that was a couple sizes too big for her. The safe house must keep some emergency clothes on hand. Willow's hair was wet from her having showered.

He stared down at his own muddy clothes. He could use a shower himself.

Her expression was somber, but she managed a smile when she saw that he was awake.

"Sorry, there's not much to eat. I can try to piece something together."

"Let me grab a quick shower and then I'll join you."

"Okay," she said. "I'll have my coffee and wait for you."

His phone jangled. It was a text from Agent Linman saying they had a new safe house set up and that transport would be there to pick Willow up within the hour. "Looks like we have a little bit of time before they come for you."

"Only for me? Aren't you going with me?"

"I can if you want me to...to the safe house anyway." He was honored that she wanted him to stay with her.

"It'll take a while for them to set you up in witness protection. Then your contact and transport person will be a US Marshal."

Her face blanched. She turned away from him and gripped the counter. "I guess that's how it has to be." She grabbed the coffee pot with a jerky motion and poured some into a cup.

He rushed over to her and placed a supportive hand on her shoulder. She pivoted and fell into his arms. While he held her, the memory of the kiss they'd shared was still foremost on his mind. They both were losing so much. Could they have been more than friends? Now he would never know.

He held her until she pulled away and then he went upstairs to shower and see if he could at least find a clean shirt. It felt like his heart had been split down the middle.

Willow sat and drank her coffee, trying not to think about the life ahead for her. She probably wouldn't be able to continue doing her photography professionally. Even that would be taken from her. The sun was shining through the pulled slats of the blinds.

She'd finished her coffee by the time Quentin came downstairs wearing a different shirt and pants that were a little short on him. She poured him a cup of coffee. "I can open a can of peaches, and there's some packaged pastry in the cupboard."

He lifted his cup. "I'll just have the coffee. Maybe we can stop and grab a bite somewhere."

She popped the pastry into the toaster. By the time she was done eating it, Quentin's phone indicated he had another text. "He's waiting outside for us."

Willow took a deep breath. She had the same feeling she'd gotten when she had to drive to a funeral. This was a death of sorts. The death of her old life. The death of the possibility of there being anything between her and Quentin.

He stood by the door waiting for her. A soft smile graced his face, but she saw the dullness in his eyes. Until that moment, she hadn't thought about her and Quentin mending things to the point where they might think about dating. No point in thinking about it now. At least she had the memory of the kiss and all that they had shared years ago.

She was still wrestling with accepting being taken into protection. "Would you ever be able to come and visit me?"

"That might put you in danger," he said.

"Why don't you have to go into witness protection?" She walked toward the door. "He tried to kill you too and now he knows you are with the law."

"I'm a trained agent. I can protect myself. You're the one who has the power to testify against him in court." He opened the door. "I'm glad though that you would want me to come visit."

She could see Agent Linman waiting outside for them. This might be her only chance to tell him how she felt. "I think we would have been friends again… and maybe something more." They stepped outside. Her mind registered the warmth of the sun on her face and then everything seemed to move in slow motion.

Agent Linman crumpled to the ground like a soda can being stepped on. A car zoomed past, its motor revving to dangerous speeds. Another shot was fired. The door of the safe house was left ajar.

She heard Quentin yell at her to get to the car. She had no recollection of running, only that she found herself in the passenger's seat. Agent Linman had risen to his feet though he was doubled over. Quentin swung open the back door so Linman could fall on the seat. Then he got in the car.

Agent Linman grimaced in pain and held his shoulder where he must've been hit.

"We'll get you to the hospital." Quentin said hitting the gas and backing out.

Agent Linman spoke through gritted teeth. "I'll be all right. Bullet barely grazed me. It's just the shock. This is your chance to catch him. White sedan."

Quentin pressed the accelerator.

Agent Linman pulled his gun from the holster with his uninjured arm. He looked at Willow.

Willow shook her head in disbelief. "How did he find us?"

"Hard to say," Quentin said. "Call the city police. Tell them we were shot at and the car drove off." He watched the street up ahead. "I should be able to tell where they are headed here in a minute as soon as I spot them."

Willow dialed 911 and explained what was going on. "We're on Thomas Street headed south."

Linman spoke from the back seat. "My guess is they are headed toward the Harris Street exit. That will get them out of town the fastest."

Willow relayed that information to the 911 operator. He promised to notify highway patrol.

Linman had leaned forward and was watching the streets. "There."

The sedan was stopped at a red light with three cars between them.

Her heart was racing. "Do you think he knows we followed him?"

"He shot twice then zoomed away which suggests to me that this was a last-ditch effort, but he didn't want to risk being caught."

She wondered if it was Mr. Smith or just the guy who had been with him from the beginning.

The light changed. Quentin hung back, keeping several cars between them. They wove through the city until they came to the exit for the highway. When they had been on the highway for several miles, she saw the highway patrol behind them. He must have been tucked away on a shoulder catching speeders.

They rounded a curve. The highway patrol was no longer visible. Up ahead the white car did a sudden turn without signaling.

What was he doing? Quentin followed.

"This might be a trap."

"Could be, or maybe he doesn't realize we tailed him. But it's our last chance." They were immediately on a winding road. A dilapidated sign indicated they were headed toward Western Town. She had a vague memory of the place being a tourist trap, filled with gift shops and a museum housed in a replica of an Old West fort.

The road wound up into the mountains. They came to what was at one time a gravel parking lot though it was overgrown. A dusty for sale or lease sign stood outside the fort. There was no sign of the white sedan.

Quentin looked all around. "This road dead-ends. He parked somewhere around here."

"I have a rifle in the back," said Agent Linman.

"I'll take that. You're probably better off with the handgun." He looked at Willow. "Call and let them know where we are. Highway patrol has probably sped past by now. You lock all the doors and stay low."

She nodded. The two men got out and approached the exterior of the fort which was made of rough-hewn logs. They exchanged some hand signals and then split off. Quentin went inside the fort, and Linman circled around the outside. Willow locked all the doors and then reached for the phone.

Before she could dial the number, the driver's side window shattered. She looked into the face of the man she had known as Mr. Smith. With a gun pointed at her, he reached in and unlocked the door.

"I suggest you slide across the seat and come out nice and slow. If you choose to fight, I'll shoot you on the spot. You might be useful to me…for a few minutes anyway."

The only reason he would have shown himself so blatantly was because he was going to kill her. Her choice was to die now or die in a few minutes. Willow complied. Once she was out of the car Mr. Smith grabbed her by the collar and jabbed the gun in her back.

From inside the fort, she heard the volley of gunfire.

Her breath caught. She prayed that Quentin had not been hit.

TWENTY-ONE

Quentin had seen the man they referred to as Yellow-shirt for just a second as he ran from the roof of one Old West building to another before he took cover. Quentin had taken a single shot, and the suspect returned fire. Quentin dove for cover behind a trough, raised the rifle and took aim again where the last shot had come from.

He heard a groan and shuffling. Had he hit his target?

He remained crouched behind the trough.

"I think you better put that rifle down right now."

Quentin turned to see the source of the voice. It hadn't come from the roof. When he turned, a man who must be Kirk Simonson was holding Willow at gunpoint.

"Drop the rifle or she takes a fatal bullet."

Willow's expression communicated fear. They were both going to die here. It was just a matter of minutes. All he could do was buy time.

"Sure." He put the rifle off to the side but remained crouched. The rifle was within arm's reach.

Kirk shouted up toward the roof. "Wren, are you okay?"

"I been hit. I been hit real bad."

The information seemed to take the wind out of Kirk's sails. His gaze darted up to the roof and then over to Quentin as if he was trying to decide what to do.

Where was Agent Linman? Certainly he had heard the shots and come running, unless he had already been taken out of the picture, either knocked unconscious or worse.

"How bad are you hit?" Kirk kept his eyes on Quentin.

Wren sounded as if he was fighting for breath between each word. "I need a doctor fast."

Kirk drew his focus back to Quentin. "Stand up and put your hands in the air." There was even more urgency in Kirk's voice.

They had only seconds to live. Quentin's mind raced as he got to his feet.

Kirk continued to grip Willow by the collar so tight she lifted her chin. The fabric must be digging into her neck. He transferred the gun from Willow's back to her temple.

Quentin was at least ten feet away from Willow. Her eyes were filled with pure terror. Willow made a "come to me" gesture with her hand. They had only one very risky choice and she was willing to do it.

He took a running leap toward Kirk. Willow knew full well if Kirk reacted fast enough, he would have time to pull the trigger and shoot her. In the same moment Quentin lunged, Willow grabbed the front of her collar so she wouldn't be choked and twisted her torso.

She didn't break free, but the move was enough to distract Kirk for a moment. Quentin reached for the hand that held the gun.

Willow punched Kirk's stomach. He dropped the gun, and Quentin moved in to restrain him.

Gunfire came from the roof where Wren was. He must have rallied enough to fire a shot. Willow dropped to the ground as more shots were fired.

Quentin fell to the ground, taking Kirk with him. Another shot whizzed over them. Kirk crawled toward the gun. Quentin managed to restrain Kirk's hand before he got to the gun, but he landed a punch to Quentin's head with his free hand. Quentin blinked from the blow and let go of Kirk's other hand.

Willow moved in beside him holding a wagon wheel spoke.

"Willow, get down. You'll be shot."

Kirk's fingers were inches from the gun when Willow hit it with the spoke. And then hit his head enough to incapacitate him. He lay still on the ground, his face turned to the side.

"Get something to tie him up with." While Willow looked around for something to secure Kirk with, Quentin grabbed the gun and aimed it toward the high building.

Wren was visible at the edge of the roof. He collapsed on his stomach, dropping the gun to the ground below.

In the distance, Quentin heard the sound of the highway patrol approaching.

Everything was going to be okay. They'd caught the infamous Mr. Smith. Willow could go back to her life in Little Horse. He had no idea what that meant for the two of them. In the moment when she had had the gun to her head and he thought he might lose her, he knew he still loved her.

He had no idea how she felt about him.

TWENTY-TWO

Willow breathed a sigh of relief when two highway patrol officers, a man and a woman, burst through the gates of the Old West fort. After Quentin explained what had happened, they took Mr. Smith into custody.

When they stepped outside to where their car was, an ambulance was making its way up the road. They found Linman in the back seat of the car pressing his hand against his injured shoulder. "I lost more blood than I realized. I had to come back here and call an ambulance before I collapsed. So sorry I let you down."

"No problem," said Quentin. "I appreciate your help." He looked toward Willow. "And your help as well."

His gaze caused a spark of electricity to shoot through her. What now? Less than an hour ago, she was adjusting to losing her entire life, including any connection to Quentin.

Quentin made sure Linman and Wren were safely loaded into the ambulance. Both it and the highway patrol car drove away, leaving her alone with the man she'd once loved. Once loved? Still loved?

They stood a few feet apart by the car. A rush of wind caused the trees surrounding the fort to creak. Her hair fluttered in the breeze.

Quentin took a step toward her. "You ready to go home?"

She nodded as a lump formed in her throat. "How about you? Are you ready to go back to your old life in Little Horse?"

"I never should have left in the first place. I'm not running anymore."

"We both ran away in one way or another. I know we can't go back to the way it was before the accident, but maybe…we could be more than friends."

He gathered her into his arms. "I was hoping you'd say that. I love you. I never stopped loving you."

She relished the warmth of his embrace. "Quentin, I love you too. I think we can repair this."

She pulled back to look into his eyes.

"I think we can do better than that. I would really love for us to work toward the wedding we intended to have five years ago. Willow, I'd like nothing more in this world than to be married to you."

Her heart fluttered. "Quentin, I love the idea of being your wife."

He rested his hand on her cheek. "Will you marry me?"

As she looked into the depth of his eyes, she knew this was what was meant to be. There had just been a detour. "Yes."

He leaned in to kiss her. She felt warm and alive. There had always been only one right person for her, and she was so glad to be in his arms again.

* * * * *

*If you enjoyed this story,
look for these other books by Sharon Dunn:*

Alaskan Christmas Target
Undercover Threat

Dear Reader,

I hope you enjoyed the adventure and the danger that Willow and Quentin faced together. As always with my books, the characters are on two journeys at the same time. One is the quest for justice and that men or women who have stepped outside the law will be captured and punished for their wrongdoing. The other is the journey of the heart that Willow and Quentin must take. They both have suffered great loss, and in their pain, they hurt each other seemingly beyond repair. But God was in their story from the start. I love writing stories that are about redemption and learning to forgive others and ourselves for the mistakes of the past. As Christians, we try to do the right thing but don't always succeed. We make mistakes. We learn to forgive. I am so glad that God is always in our story.

Sincerely
Sharon Dunn

COMING NEXT MONTH FROM
Love Inspired Suspense

DANGEROUS MOUNTAIN RESCUE
K-9 Search and Rescue • by Christy Barritt

Erin Lansing will search every inch of the mountains to find her teen daughter who has disappeared—even if someone is intent on stopping her at all costs. Teaming up with search-and-rescue K-9 handler Dillon Walker and his dog, Scout, might be her only chance at seeing her daughter again...and staying alive.

DEATH VALLEY DOUBLE CROSS
Desert Justice • by Dana Mentink

As family secrets surface, Pilar Jefferson must unravel the mystery of her supposedly deceased father in order to find her missing mother—and escape an assassin. But when her ex-fiancé, Austin Duke, gets pulled into the investigation, will they survive long enough for her to tell him the real reason she fled on their wedding day?

SMUGGLERS IN AMISH COUNTRY
by Debby Giusti

Tracking a robbery suspect forces Atlanta cop Marti Sommers to go undercover in an Amish community where the criminal is attacking delivery girls. When Luke Lehman's niece is threatened, Marti will have to partner with the former officer turned Amish guardian to save everyone they care about...including each other.

TEXAS COLD CASE THREAT
Quantico Profilers • by Jessica R. Patch

When a murderer sends her taunting letters, FBI behavioral analyst Chelsey Banks retreats to a friend's ranch—and interrupts the housekeeper being attacked. Learning it matches the MO of a cold-case serial killer, she'll need to work with her best friend, Texas Ranger Tack Holliday—unless one of the culprits gets her first.

SAFE HOUSE EXPOSED
by Darlene L. Turner

After a leak in the Canadian witness protection program exposes his sister-in-law and his niece, police constable Mason James races to protect them. But with a crime family hunting Emma and little Sierra, there's no safe place to hide...and nobody to trust.

TRACKING CONCEALED EVIDENCE
by Sharee Stover

Discovering Detective Shaylee Adler buried alive is only the first clue former forensic entomologist Jamie Dyer and cadaver dog Bugsy unearth. Together, they'll have to untangle the connections between Shaylee's missing sister, her senator brother-in-law and the person now hunting them all.

———

LOOK FOR THESE AND OTHER LOVE INSPIRED BOOKS WHEREVER BOOKS ARE SOLD, INCLUDING MOST BOOKSTORES, SUPERMARKETS, DISCOUNT STORES AND DRUGSTORES.

LISCNM0122B

"He's brazen. He parked right behind Izzy's old van knowing there was a possibility of someone—maybe even me—seeing it." Which she had. She could kick herself for not getting the tag number.

"Are you saying I'm looking for an arrogant killer who loves the thrill of almost getting caught but believes he won't because he's uncatchable?"

Her past mistakes told her not to make a solid conclusion so soon, but this guy had proved more than once what kind of man he was, what kind of killer. Still, she hesitated to give Tack a profile that would aid in his search. "Perhaps," she said as a knot pinched in her gut.

"Perhaps? Chelsey, give me something I can work with."

Chelsey drank the ice water, letting it cool her burning throat. What if she was wrong? "I'm not ready to spin what little thread we have into a tapestry yet." She could not have another profile backfiring. Another stain on her previously impeccable record. Lives depended on it. Tack's career depended on it. The last thing Chelsey wanted was Tack's name being smeared because of his connection with Chelsey and her profession.

Or her personal stains that could smear him.

"Agents—" a hospital security officer stepped inside "—we have a media frenzy outside. They want more information on this Outlaw. They know a woman died at his hands. In our care."

The Outlaw. Chelsey's name for him.

The only other person besides Tack who knew she'd called him that was Juan. He must have talked to the press after he left the hospital. So much for not letting their personal nickname for him get out. Now they were here wanting answers. She didn't have a single one.

"We're going to have to go out there, Chels," Tack said. "Me and you. Working a case together. Who would have thought."

And now if anything at all were amiss, Tack would go down with an already sinking ship in the form of his oldest and dearest friend.

What had she gotten him into? And could she get him out?

Don't miss
Texas Cold Case Threat by Jessica R. Patch,
available March 2022 wherever
Love Inspired Suspense books and ebooks are sold.

And look for a new extended-length novel from
Jessica R. Patch, Her Darkest Secret,
coming soon from Love Inspired!

LoveInspired.com

IF YOU ENJOYED THIS BOOK, DON'T MISS NEW EXTENDED-LENGTH NOVELS FROM LOVE INSPIRED!

In addition to the Love Inspired books you know and love, we're excited to introduce even more uplifting stories in a longer format, with more inspiring fresh starts and page-turning thrills!

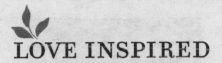

LOVE INSPIRED

Stories to uplift and inspire.

Fall in love with Love Inspired—inspirational and uplifting stories of faith and hope. Find strength and comfort in the bonds of friendship and community. Revel in the warmth of possibility, and the promise of new beginnings.

LOOK FOR THESE LOVE INSPIRED TITLES ONLINE AND IN THE BOOK DEPARTMENT OF YOUR FAVORITE RETAILER!

**With her family's legacy on the line,
a woman with everything to lose must rely
on a man hiding from his past...**

Don't miss this thrilling and uplifting page-turner from
New York Times bestselling author

LINDA GOODNIGHT

"Linda Goodnight has a true knack for writing historical Western
fiction, with characters who come off the pages with life."
—**Jodi Thomas**, *New York Times* and *USA TODAY* bestselling author

Coming soon from Love Inspired!

LoveInspired.com

LI41876BPA